AF417042

ODDITY OF LOVE

MARQUIS DE SADE .. THE MAN FROM WHOM SADISM GOT ITS NAME

We have all heard the term sadism, which can be defined simply as the pleasure one gets from causing physical and psychological pain and harm to others and is often associated with sexual relationships, and most of us might think that this term is Arabic, but it is not, it happens on behalf of the Marquis François, his life was full of adventure and scandal, which led him to spend many years of his life in prison, during which he wrote several pornographic novels about sadism and violence associated with sex, and called for atheism and rejection of morality. therefore his books are banned in most countries of the world.

Tyrannical, evil, extremist in everything with an insatiable imagination, lustful and keen to fanaticism, this is how the Marquis de Sade describes himself in one of his last letters, a brief description of a wild and stormy life that rebelled against everything and became for some a companion of vice and Perversion. and for others it has the title of liberation from the constraints that fetter the human soul, a life that was a manifestation of wild and irregular desires that seethed in the minds and imaginations of most people, but it is usually curbed by the whip of tradition, morality and religion. As for the Marquis de

Sade and others like him, they give them the will to act as you want.

Alphonse François de Sade was born on June 2, 1740 in one of the French royal palaces. His family came from one of the oldest and oldest French aristocratic families. He studied as a child with his uncle Abe de Sade, who was an intellectual tycoon and then went to school for sons of the noble class to complete his studies, and at the age of fifteen he enlisted in the army in the royal light cavalry class and fought in the the time of the seven years' war that broke out between the great powers of Europe at that time, and he proved his bravery in the arena of war. He was afraid and rose to the rank of colonel at the age of nineteen. In 1763, the Marquis left Diye, the army gained the upper hand and returned to Paris as a handsome young man seeking pleasure and pleasure, and Paris was not a utopia at the time, but his palaces were full of news of sex parties The dignity and betrayal of husbands and wives, and he himself the court was a breeding ground for moral decay, since the king took beautiful women from the hands of their husbands to become his concubines and mistresses, and Madame de Pompadour was the most famous in this field., and court women took lovers to satisfy their whims, while the Conflict due to men did not become like a bet and a challenge, and although the punishment for homosexuality reached the death penalty, the relationship of homosexuality and lesbianism was widespread among members of high society, and sexual stimulants and means of sexual entertainment were known and popular, and as a result the French state was infected with financial and moral corruption that spread to the Church and was the main reason the growing hatred of the people for the aristocracy. as at the time when these people were having fun and playing, people suffered under the weight of hunger and poverty, and as a result, revolutionary ideas and beliefs of disbelief and atheism spread, bars and brothels of prostitution and moral decay spread, and the Marquis de Sade lived in this society, and his rough and lustful romances were a reflection of the type of life and culture that was popular in Paris, he mixed it with imagination and smelled of blood.

And in order to save him from the nightlife and the embrace of Parisian prostitutes, his family decided to marry him to Rene de Mentreuil, the daughter of one of the wealthy bourgeois families, who admired the handsome young marquis and immediately agreed to him, and the couple lived in a palace near Paris. but the marriage did not change anything in the character of the marquis. Soon, news of his sex scandals began to spread and became in every language. He spent most of his time in brothels, and his sexual relations were not only with women, but also with men, and many prostitutes complained about his mistreatment of them. He likes to harm and torture them, so he was detained and imprisoned for a short time, and the police warned all brothels in Paris about the dangers of doing business with him. In 1768, he invited a poor girl named Rosa Keeler to his palace under the pretext of helping her, where he imprisoned her, whipped her and raped her. Melted wax poured her body, and the girl was able to get rid of the marquis by jumping out of a window on the second floor of the palace and in panic ran away to report to the police, and although de Sade persuaded her with money to abandon her case against him, the government decided to deport the marquis from Paris and send him to live far away in his castle at de Lacoste, in the south of France. In the castle, the marquis lived with his wife, who loved him, so she protected him and covered him, despite the fact that she knew about his actions, and in 1771 his wife's sister came to visit them, she was a young woman and a virgin. living in a convent to become a nun, and soon de Sade plunged her into his strings and established a relationship with her, the first purpose of which was to anger his mother-in-law with whom he had a bad relationship, and de Sade continued in his madness and divorced him., and in 1772 he threw a rowdy sex party, which included four prostitutes in addition to his servant Latour, who had an abnormal sexual relationship with him, and the marquis used some strong powders as sexual stimulants, which led to the poisoning of one of the girls , so he was sentenced to death for using poison in addition to engaging in sodomy, but the Marquis managed to escape to Italy before his arrest, and He accompanied his wife's sister and servant Latour, and he was are stovan in Italy after a while and imprisoned with his servant in one of the fortresses., while his wife's sister took refuge in a monastery and remained there until the end of her life. The Marquis de Sade did not spend long in captivity, as soon as he and his servant managed to get out of the fort, leaving in the cell a letter addressed to the jailers, in which he thanked them for their good treatment and wished they would not be punished for his escape, and returned to his castle in Lacoste to live in hiding and continue his lustful life with the help of his wife, who loved him to such an extent that she was ready to forgive him everything. She hired many beautiful servants and beautiful maids to please her husband, who did not get bored or tired of shameless group sex parties, attended by girls and boys, during which all forms of homosexuality, including homosexuality , were practiced . And lesbianism, and group sex, and sadism, accompanied by beating with whips, putting bridles on their mouths, and putting handcuffs on hands and feet, and other methods in which the marquis succeeded and wrote about in his pornographic stories and novels, and because of of this madness, accompanied by madness, most of those who worked for the Marquis were His wives, quickly fled due to their persecution, and sometimes rape, and some of the actions of the Marquis were so disgusting that in 1777 the father of one of the girls who worked in the castle, came and tried to kill the Marquis, but, fortunately for the latter, the pistol did not fire.

In 1778, a letter came to the castle, in which the marquis informed that his mother was sick and dying, and when he went to visit her in Paris, he found that she had died and was arrested, the ambush was arranged by his mother-in-law, who never forgave to him that he seduced her youngest daughter and took her with him to Italy, and the marquis was imprisoned in the Château de Vincennes and managed to escape from there, but he was soon arrested again and returned to his prison to spend several years writing his pornographic novels, and in 1784 he was transferred to the famous Prison of the Bastille, where De Sade wrote some of his most famous novels, among them "120 days in Sodom or the school of debauchery" and "Justine" and "Juliet", and it is said that the Marquis was one of the reasons for the first spark of the French revolution against the monarchy in 1789, as while Paris was seething with anger, de Sade shouted from his cell At the roaring crowd outside, saying: "Prisoners are being killed here!" And only days passed before the revolution and pad the Bastille.

The Marquis de Sade was released from prison in 1790 only to find that everything around him had changed, his two sons and daughter became young people who barely knew him, and his wife asked for a divorce and got him, so he became lonely, but he did not feel sad, on the contrary, he felt comfortable to get rid of family ties. And he turned into a purebred revolutionary despite his aristocratic background, which is why he called himself a "citizen of the prevailing" and lived in Paris, because his castle in Lacoste was destroyed by an angry mob during the revolution and he met an unknown actress named Marie Questance Quisne , whose husband abandoned her, leaving her with a small child At the age of six, they lived together, and only death separated them, and the marquis began to get involved in political life and joined revolutionary committees, and then was elected a member of the French National Assembly., and despite his position in relation to the revolution and his support for it, many looked at him On the grounds that he was a former aristocrat, his position worsened with the enrollment of his son in the ranks of opponents of the revolution, and in 1793 he was removed from office and accused of anti-revolutionary and imprisoned during the Terror (Reign of Terror), during which thousands of Frenchmen were executed by the stroke of the pen ava of the public safety committee of serial killer Maximilian Robespierre, but it looks like the marquis's neck eluded the guillotine due to an error in the records and in 1794 Robespierre was killed and the period of terror ended and the marquis was released, whose financial affairs began deteriorate, and he was forced in 1796 to sell the ruins of his castle and estate in Lacoste at a low price, and during the years after the revolution he continued to write his pornographic novels in addition to some political novels. He also made several performances for some of his plays, some of which were successful and well received among the French public.

In 1801, Napoleon Bonaparte ordered the arrest of the man who wrote the novels Justine and Juliet, and put him in prison, regardless of whether he was there, without trial, so the Marquis de Sade was arrested and imprisoned in Paris, but soon he was transferred to another prison because of his attempt to seduce a prisoner. Young. In 1803, his family declared him insane and arranged so that he was released from prison and placed in a psychiatric hospital, and his mistress Mary Kcssna was allowed to live with him, since she claimed that she was his daughter, and in the sanatorium the Marquis continued to compose his novels and presented some of his plays, since he never stopped researching sexual pleasure, despite reaching the age of seventy. In his will, de Sade ordered that his body be left in the room in which he died for 48 hours without touching, and then transferred to one of his estates to be buried there, despite his atheism and rejection of any religious manifestations at his funeral. his family brought a priest to pray over him and put a cross on his grave, and the grave was opened decades later and his skull was taken for study in the science of reading skulls (an ancient theory completely rejected by modern science based on the premise that the shape human skull affects his behavior and behavior), and after the death of the Marquis, his eldest son burned all his papers, which contained many novels and plays that were not published, as well as his family, changing his last name, and to this day he avoids most of the descendants de Sade to mention any connection they had with him.

Although most of his works and writings were lost after his death, some of them survived, especially those that were printed during the life of the Marquis, and the most famous of them are:

- 120 days in Sadoma, or the school of immorality: this is the most expensive novel of the Marquis, which he wrote during his imprisonment in the Bastille, and he hid it in the lists of a family member, for fear of being confiscated by the jailers. After the revolution, enraged masses broke into the Bastille prison and plundered it. It was lost along with the rest of his writings by the rabble, but in 1904 a copy that the Marquis accidentally hid was printed and made into a film, and her story revolves around four wealthy men who lock themselves with 42 boys and girls in an isolated castle. over the mountains and invite them to the Four Leaders to talk about the sexual adventures they have experienced in their lives, and their stories inspire the four men to torture and sexually abuse boys and girls of all kinds, which ends up killing them all.

Justin: This is a young woman who commits several crimes and is sentenced to death and tells her life story to another woman. She tells her about how she was raped at thirteen years old and about the misfortune that accompanied her all her life, so she was raped and subjected to physical and sexual abuse wherever she went.

Philosophy in the room: It revolves around a fifteen-year-old girl named Eugenia, whom the family sent to educate three teachers, a woman, her brother and an hermaphrodite, and they convince the girl that morality and traditions are just lies and they teach her various sexual arts and throw shameless parties in which everyone participates, and when her mother comes to free her from their hands, they rape the mother and torture her, and the daughter enthusiastically participates in this and wants to kill her mother, so they bring a slave girl with syphilis. to rape the mother and transmit the disease to her, and then leave her to return home, dragging traces of disappointment and shame with her

And there are many other novels and plays by the Marquis de Sade that all revolve around rejecting morality, tradition and religion and allowing a person to do what they want without any restrictions, since they all involve various forms of pornography, usually associated with violence. such as rape, homosexuality, lesbianism, incest and whatever is possible. Although some of these novels have been published and translated into languages other than French, most of them are banned from distribution in most countries of the world due to the violence and sadistic ideas they contain, and this may be the only area in which the novels of the Marquis can be presented, these are pornographic films, most of which are cited in this area.

It remains to mention that the Marquis de Sade, despite the fact that he practiced physical violence and most of his stories and novels contained murder and bloodshed, but this man did not know about him, that he killed a man except on the battlefield, and he wrote about himself so: "I imagined all kinds of sins, but I certainly did not commit all of them and I will not commit them. "

Note: There is a difference between sadism and masochism (in relation to Leopold Mazuch, an Austrian writer). The sadist experiences pleasure and euphoria from hurting others. As for the masochist or masochist, he experiences pleasure from the pain inflicted on him. The Marquis de Sade loved to hurt those who had sex with him. He asks his mistress to torture and rape him, and he really likes it.

HUMAN MARRIAGES TO ANIMALS ... BETWEEN MYTHS, SCIENTIFIC FACTS AND THE PROHIBITION OF RELIGIONS

Thousands of years ago, inscriptions and huge stone drawings in the temples and palaces of some ancient civilizations told us about supernatural mythical creatures that combined human and animal features in their bodies, mythical creatures that the ancients claimed that some of them were the result of abnormal sexual relations between people and animals. Although these terrifying monsters were confined to the world of myth and myth, the sexual relationship between humans and animals was not what all nations knew it, but it was a silent relationship, shrouded in silence and surrounded by a halo of mystery, perhaps due to people's disapproval. And also because the poor have no language to complain about their wise rapists! And just as ancient man feared the superstitious monsters that resulted from these sinful relationships, civilized man today complains of the same obsession after scientists were able to create hybrid creatures in the laboratory, and who knows what they will do in the future?

Over time, I realized that sexual desire is a controlling instinct that directs a person's behavior, which sometimes upsets him and pushes him into the ranks of animals. They happen every day, and they have happened since time immemorial, but people do not like to refer to them as embarrassing, frightening or tolerant, such as incest, sex with dead bodies, rape of young children, sadism, masochism, etc., and although most of us do not like to hear these things, They frown at them, but we must remember that we are not angels. Most people sometimes have strange, strange ideas, but the good thing is that most people keep these ideas in the imagination and few of them turn them into action and action.

Between myths and history

In all ancient civilizations, there were gods and supernatural beings who combined the features of humans and animals in their bodies. In Pharaonic Egypt, for example, the sun god Ra took the form of a man with the head of a falcon, while the god of wisdom Thoth was embodied in the form of a man with the head of an ibis. As for the god of the dead and the afterlife, Anubis had the head of the son of Uy, and besides these gods, the Egypt of the Pharaohs abounded with many hybrid gods and monsters, and perhaps the most famous in this area is the Great Sphinx. These monsters were not limited to the civilization of the pharaohs, but were known to all ancient peoples, and their forms and characteristics varied, for example, Assyrian winged bulls, nymphs, centaurs ... etc., and these strange creatures were among the creations of the goddess, in while others were the product of the sexual relationship of sinners between humans and animals, for example, the Minotaur is a Greek mythical beast, embodied in ancient mythology as a man with a bull's head, and he, as legend has it, is the product of a sexual relationship between the queen of Crete and the beautiful a white bull sent by the god Poseidon as a gift to her husband, King Minos, to sacrifice him.

And apart from ancient myths, sexual relations between humans and animals were not purely mythical, rather they were sometimes practiced within the framework of religious and magical rituals and rituals. For example, a number of Greek and Roman historians have mentioned that some of the Pharaonic priestesses had sex with the sacred Capricorn (he mentioned goats raised in the temple), and that this practice had a religious dimension and was sometimes practiced openly. It seems that this practice was known and widespread in all ancient civilizations, so it was mentioned and explicitly prohibited in the Torah and the Old Testament.

In Europe, there is a stone inscription in northern Italy dating from the third millennium BC, one of its inscriptions contains an image of a man having sex with a donkey, and in Sweden archaeologists have found inscriptions depicting sexual practices in some graves dating back to the second millennium BC between man and animal. As for the Greeks, some of their sources were unequivocal about the propensity of some of their women to have sex with male caribou and how much they preferred it to men! As for the men themselves, they preferred the kid! And the Roman era was not without strange sexual practices mentioned by some historians in their books, one of which is that some women plant little snakes in their chicks for sexual pleasure, as well as to cool the body in the hot summer !!. In the Roman arena of death, animal sex took on an epic character. Historians have mentioned that the Romans had a special way of teaching certain wild animals to have sex with women and men, and they used these animals during death shows that were very popular, so they released them on women who were sacrificed inside the ring. the animal then raped them during full intercourse, and the female victim often remained after the rape to be killed by the animal, a barbaric practice that was one of the most popular and enthusiastic shows among the Roman public.

In India, there is a famous inscription on the wall of a Hindu temple depicting an Indian man openly having sex with a horse, while a woman stands next to him, covering her face with her hand in an expression of her disgust.

The Arabs also knew about sex with animals such as camels and horses, and honorable hadiths were mentioned in prohibiting and criminalizing this issue, and the funny thing is that some people in Iraq and the Gulf countries still describe a beautiful, plump woman as "nakah" which means camel!

The conclusion we draw from this brief historical summary is that the sex between man and animals was not limited to a particular nation or nation, but was known to all peoples and nations, without exception, from the most remote regions of Japan and even the pastures of the American Indian tribes. in North America.

Bestiality (bestiality) What is it and how is it called?

It is a Greek word meaning "animal love" and the first person to use the term was the scientist Kraft Ebbank in 1886, and he coined the term specifically for everything related to the field of sexual relations between humans and animals, whether full sexual relationships, that is, penetration and ejaculation, or just caress and touch, like caressing the genitals of an animal or masturbating the body of an animal, and it seems that the area of this term is rubber. This is the lust for sexual intercourse, and some of them exclude sexual relations, which are accompanied by violence, that is, sadism, and the main purpose of which is to harm the animal. Also, most researchers agree to exclude emotional relationships that arise between a person and his pet, which sometimes reach a high level of affection and love, but do not include any sexual practices.

Zoophilia is also engaged in and explores the impact of sexual practices on human and animal behavior, and, for example, whether animals can enjoy sex with humans! There are many men and women who have practiced bestiality, claiming that their animal partner enjoys sex with them, and sometimes with whoever initiates it. A dog, for example, can be trained to have sex with humans, and there are many men or women who have written about their sexual experiences with their dogs. But most researchers argue that, no matter to what extent an animal enjoys and gets used to sex with humans, it actually learned only what humans taught it, that is, the animal has no opportunity to choose and has no right to refuse and abstain. rather, one can never know if it really enjoys it, even if it seems to him that he does it.

The exact extent of bestiality is unknown and there are few small scale statistics in this area, one of the oldest such statistics was conducted in the United States in the 1940s and found that about 8% of men and 4% of women had at least once in their life, have had full or partial sexual intercourse with an animal, and that about 8% of men and 4% of women have had at least once in their life, have had full or partial sexual intercourse with an animal. But other statistics from the 1980s showed a drop in these percentages by almost half, and the reason for this is the opinion of researchers that agricultural life in America is decreasing and most rural cities are turning into urban centers, and therefore, human contact with animals has decreased by a large percentage, but a decrease in this percentage does not mean that people freely communicate with animals. , Either ashamed, or afraid of scandal and punishment.

Think online today about the most important means by which you can get prevalence rates of this phenomenon, where there are resorts and certain sites where pedophile people have sex with animals, often under pseudonyms, share stories and experiences. In the developing world, where a large number of people are still engaged in agriculture, it is very difficult to determine the extent of the prevalence of bestiality, because talking about it is sometimes limited to whispers and chuckles exchanged among rural teenagers, and, despite people's disapproval of these relationships, the degree of taboo or the taboo around them is less significant. While for many, sex with an animal may mean little more than an incident worthy of laughter and ridicule, the people who have been spotted with these homosexuals can become a scarcity spot for the rest of their lives.

There are some researchers who consider bestiality to be a psychological condition that requires treatment, and there are also those who attribute it to inhibition and sexual desire, and suppression may partially explain why this phenomenon is widespread in our Arab countries, where a conservative society imposes severe restrictions on relationships. between men and women, but this does not explain to us why this phenomenon is widespread and widespread in Western societies, and therefore most researchers in the field of bestiality believe that it is associated not only with sexual inhibition, but there are people who prefer an animal as the condition of your sexuality, because he does not remember or criticize or blur out secrets, but is faithful and obedient, and this page is often inaccessible in a human partner.

Zoophilia is also associated with health risks that can arise from sexual practices between humans and animals, and these risks can sometimes arise from animal behavior during sex that is different from human behavior and is sometimes characterized by violent movements such as biting or scratching, animals usually use their sharp claws and sometimes their fangs to avoid it. In addition, animal genital insertion is different from human genital insertion, so reckless sexual practices can lead to serious injuries and sometimes fatal bleeding, and there are many incidents in this area around the world, some of which have been fatal, especially when practiced with large animals such as horses, and there are similar incidents with dogs, because their penis can lead to serious injury. In addition to threats, physical violence, human contact with the animal's body can lead to the transmission of many dangerous diseases, for example, the seeds of an animal can be deadly vector types of viruses and bacteria that can lead to serious illness.

Opinion on religion and law in bestiality

All heavenly religions prohibit bestiality and regard it as a heinous and sinful deed that believers should not commit. It is forbidden in Judaism and Christianity, where there is an explicit reference to bestiality in the Old Testament of the Bible. :

(23:18): and do not do your rottenness with the Beast and do not defile it. A woman does not stand in front of a woman. It is obscene. (15:20): if a person goes to bed with the beast, he will kill, and the beast will die. (16:20): If the woman gets close to the hippo, the woman and the hippo will die. They kill. Their blood is on them.

In Islam, there are no explicit verses in the Qur'an that touch upon the topic of bestiality, but Muslims in general and in various doctrines and schools agree on the prohibition and study of this issue and are derived in the prohibition of some hadiths, as well as some jurisprudence of the imams of Islamic doctrines.

In India, some Hindu schools prohibit bestiality, and those who practice it can be severely punished, especially in the case of the desecration of sacred cows.

Buddhism also prohibits bestiality and considers it just as harmful to oneself and others as adultery, murder and rape.

In addition to the prohibition of religions, the laws of some countries of the civilized world consider bestiality a crime that can lead to a punishment of imprisonment, as in the laws of Canada, the Netherlands, Australia and New Zealand, as well as in most US states, and there are countries where there is no explicit mentions of bestiality in their laws, but prohibits and punishes it, as in Peru, for example, one man is forbidden to have a female alpaca (llama-like animal) in his house.

The prevention and prohibition of zoophilia in laws is primarily related to the degree of the state's commitment to basic animal rights and the degree of activity of groups defending these rights on their territory, so most Western countries prohibit zoophilia and consider it a crime worthy of punishment.

Could bestiality lead to the birth of hybrid creatures?

After we learned that sex between humans and animals has been possible and practiced by humans since ancient times, many of us may wonder about the possibility that the hybrid mythical creatures mentioned in ancient myths could be real and that they could exist. in the old days? Is it possible that sexual relations between humans and animals lead to the birth of a hybrid creature that carries the traits of both parents? To answer this question, we first need to know what a hybrid is and how to reproduce hybrids between different animal species.

In general, a hybrid can be defined as the offspring resulting from the mating of animals or plants belonging to different species, strains or families within the general classification of living organisms, and this mixed mating can occur spontaneously in nature, as can be from human control with the purpose of selecting and rooting the best traits in animals or plants that he crosses.

In general, hybrids can be produced in the following situations:

This can happen between two different subspecies, as in the case of Siberian tiger mating with Bengal tiger. - This can happen as a result of mating of two different species (Species) within the same sex (Genus), an example of this is the mating of a tiger and a lion. - It can happen, on rare occasions, between two different genders (Genera), an example of this is a sheep and a goat (Meta is often born) - It can happen, but very rarely, as a result of mixed marriages between two different families (Families).

Except for the above cases, it is generally unknown, and it may be impossible to give birth to a hybrid in vivo, belonging to two different ranks (Order), or to a classification above the rank, and therefore it is impossible, for example, to give birth to a hybrid creature as a result of sexual intercourse between a person and the dog, because they belong to two different ranks, and also because of the difference in the number of chromosomes (genetic pigment) that each carries, so that a person has 46 chromosomes, and a dog has 78 chromosomes.

But if we are talking about chromosomes, then is it possible under normal conditions to produce a hybrid between a person who has (46) chromosomes in his cells, and between a rabbit

(44) or a mouse (42), and the answer, of course, is negative, because they belong to different ranks, but you can produce a hybrid by mating a donkey (62) with a horse (64), because they are of the same race and rank, and the newborn will be a mule and will have 63 chromosomes and, therefore, will be sterile.

There is only one case that should theoretically lead to a hybrid being in vivo, and that case is human mating with chimpanzees, since both belong to the great apes family and are close in chromosome number and have the same genetic map. there are many stories throughout history that speak of the birth of such a hybrid, for example, one European historian of the 11th century mentioned the story of a nobleman who had sexual relations with monkeys, and that this monkey was very jealous when one day saw him sleeping in the arms of His wife, who killed him, and the European historian claimed that the apes later gave birth to a hybrid creature and that he himself saw it. Of course, there is no evidence to support the authenticity of this story, but we mentioned it as an example of the belief of medieval people in the possibility of sex with abilities and procreation from this connection. Arab zoologists in the Middle Ages warned women in their books against exposing their bodies or nudity in front of male monkeys, because they claim that human women crave sex. In the modern era, especially at the beginning of the last century, a number of Soviet and European scientists tried to fertilize female chimpanzees with human sperm and tried to fertilize some female volunteers with chimpanzee sperm, but in both cases, failure was their ally, and pregnancy did not occur.

There is only one case in the world of a chimpanzee named Oliver, which scientists suspect is a hybrid due to its strange shape, behavior and human gait. The reliability of the DNA test results is questioned, and many still believe that this is a true hybrid of a human and a chimpanzee.

The wisdom of the difference in the number of chromosomes between living organisms is that the races do not overlap with each other. Therefore, hybrid genera between different races and species are rare and often sterile. In addition, the convergence of the number of chromosomes of mouse, rabbit and monkey with a human being made it the most used in medical laboratories to conduct experiments on it, because it is closest to it genetically, but scientists today are thinking about creating a hybrid in laboratory conditions that they could would be used in their experiments to revolutionize the world of medicine and health.

Parahuman ... the science behind humans

For several decades, scientists have been conducting genetic experiments with the aim of producing hybrid animals carrying some human characteristics and characteristics in order to benefit from them in their scientific and medical research, for example, by producing animal hybrids that have a heart, lungs or a human kidney, millions of lives , annually lost all over the world due to the lack of alternative organs, will be saved. For example, research aimed at treating AIDS can be developed and advanced by creating mice with immune systems similar to the human immune system. Likewise, a cure can be found for diseases such as diabetes, Parkinson's, and Alzheimer's (dementia).

Despite all of the aforementioned noble goals, transhumanism research by scholars is facing strong opposition from clergy and politicians, and even from some scholars and academics, many ethical questions arise on this topic, which many see as an insult to human dignity, for example, what is will the fate of the hybrid creatures be if they are indeed bred, and how will they be treated? Will he be considered human or will he be classified under a new species? Will it give the right to procreation and reproduction, and will you understand the reasons that prompted people to build it in such a distorted way? And how will a person behave if these hybrid creatures get out of his control?

In fact, the controversy on this topic concerns not only the production and generation of complete hybrid creatures, but also extends to the request of scientists to allow them to create hybrid embryos in laboratories for research purposes. For example, scientists from Newcastle University and King's College in the UK have applied for a permit for the 2006 period. Three years to create human and animal embryos, provided that the embryos will be used in stem cell research and are not allowed to grow for more than 14 days, that is, their size will not exceed the tip of a feather, and the goal is to extract the stem cells from a six day old embryo and then destroy them. Stem cells are immature cells that are capable of transforming into any type of tissue in the body, which scientists hope to use to produce human organs and treat certain diseases. This request was met with strong opposition from various sectors of public opinion, so the government was forced to reject it, but it came back and allowed it in 2007, fearing that the ban would delay the UK in this future area of research compared to countries such as China and Canada.

Despite the insistence of scientific institutions specializing in genetics and genetic research that their research is limited only to the field of hybrid embryos, many around the world are suspicious of these claims. Who knows what unethical experiments developed countries are conducting in their secret laboratories, and who knows what will happen in the future and how long scientists will be able to curb their endless curiosity in exploring the depths of this dangerous scientific field, and perhaps the day will come when hybrid creatures will live with us on Earth and become the inevitable reality of fighting it, lest it become strange that a person leaves the house in the morning to greet his neighbor who owns a cow's udder and grazes grass in the garden. or on his neighbor who has a flying wing, he moves with them to his workplace away from traffic and vehicles !!

Important note: The purpose of this article is not to arouse desires, and for those looking for these things, the internet is filled with the dirtiest things imaginable by the mind, and when I write, I assume that those who read my articles are adults because What I know from experience is that most teenagers do not exhaust themselves with a few lines of reading, let alone a multi-page article. I would also like to show that I have almost no knowledge of biology and genetics, so if any of the readers find an error in their translation, please warn me so that I can correct it, and I will be grateful.

WHAT DO YOU KNOW ABOUT MASOCHISM?

Sex plays an important role in guiding human behavior, according to the founder of the School of Modern Psychoanalysis Sigmund Freud (1) .. No, he even controls the weather and rain, according to the theory of a strange psychiatrist named Wilhelm Reich (2) - and this is another story, to which we can return in the coming days - !!! And even the celestial religions all realized the importance of sex in life, so no matter how a person tries to disobey this fact and is blind to it, hiding behind the clothes of virtue and decency, the instinct will reach his head like a demon to indulge his life every day, he trying to curb it while she struggles to get him to surrender and depend on her so that you see this poor person in conflict Always, He walks the path of suffering and dares to plunge into distress and conduct himself and others unnecessarily or needlessly at all these troubles. What he tries to deny and dry out is in his body, there is no jaw or escape from it, but this overwhelming instinct and suffocating lust can eventually lead - in addition to other factors - to things that may not happen. This stems from anomalies, rape, incest, violence and accumulated psychological knots .. so on. And please, here, that the reader does not put these words in place or deviate from their clear purpose, as this is not an invitation to sexual porn, but rather an invitation to enjoy a healthy and normal sex life. However, I am fully aware - especially since I belong to a generation dominated by mental illness as it struggles to inherit his contract and disruptions to a new generation! That family, society and traditions play an important role in shaping the personality and behavior of an Arab person.

The bottom line is that sexual culture is necessary to educate new young people, especially in our current era, when sexual temptations and stimuli look in the head from everywhere, songs, TV shows, films, commercial advertisements and the web page .. Etc. , it is good to know some things in this area that affect a person's life and thoughts, and there is no harm in defining some terms and meanings related to gender that many may not know about, especially those that have a lot of weirdness and anomalies, then there are those that fall under the jurisdiction of our site Interested in strangeness and miracles. Rather, it can be a double benefit in addressing these issues, so those who have doubts and suspicions about some of their sexual orientation know the truth about what they are suffering from, and this issue can be corrected with psychological counseling.

What is masochism?

Masochism - also called masochism or masochism - (Sexual masochism) It is simply the feeling of arousal and orgasm when receiving pain, torture and humiliation from another, and it is gender related and classified under homosexuality (Paraphilia) 3) It is the opposite of sadism. While Sadie is thrilled and relishing the pain of her sexual partner, the masochist is provoked and happy to receive pain. But in order for a person to be described as a masochist, the pain must be real, that is, accompanied by an act, and not just fantasies and desires, for example, that a wife asks her husband to hit and beat her during sex, and she does not feel pleasure and orgasm, except when doing these things, and vice versa, that is, asking a husband to his wife was tortured and humiliated for the same purpose.

A masochist usually receives pain from another person, and this person or sexual partner may be an ordinary and natural person who tortures the masochist at his request, and in other cases, the sexual partner may be sadistic, that is, he likes to direct pain to others during sexual practice, and in this case it is called Sodomazochism (Sadomasochism (And between the two parties there is often a preliminary agreement, that is, the sadist and the masochist are in their roles, that is, the one who directs the pain and the one who receives it, therefore this practice usually accompanied by some preparations where certain sexual instruments are used, such as shackles, chains, whips, sex toys, and muzzle) etc. The practice may also include psychological aspects such as a sadist playing the role of Mr. Master at the time as a masochist imagines the role of a servant or servant (Slave.) But masochism does not always require the presence of a sexual partner, sometimes the masochist directs pain to himself through the skin , stabs or burns. Etc. during masturbation or exclusivity (4)..

Not all sexual practices between partners in bed are classified as masochistic or sadistic. For example, in the normal case, most men are sadistic, and most women are masochistic, that is, women surrender and submit to men during sex due to the nature of the physical and emotional formation of both parties, and this state is normal and normal if it occurs within the framework of understanding. friendliness and love, such as biting, touching up and gently pulling hair ... Etc. is not classified as sadistic or masochistic unless it includes an urgent and constant desire to use and direct pain or receive it from a sexual partner.

What is general masochism?

General Masochism (Masochistic Personality Disorder) It is not related to sex, but it is classified as one of the cases of what psychology calls self-destructive behavior (Self-destructive behavior) A person must do something or put himself in a situation where he may know in advance, that she will return to him with failure, deprivation and humiliation, yet this person finds pleasure and hidden consolation in these things, that is, he loves to represent the role of the victim, oppressed and disadvantaged, despite his complaint and obvious complaint about it, and from forms of public masochism

- He refused to help him others and said that this help is useless. - If positive events occur in his life, it makes him feel guilty. He provokes others - because of his actions - to reject him or be angry with him, and then he feels resentful and ostracized. - He rejects the opportunities he has to rejoice and enjoy, despite the fact that he has the capabilities and qualifications. to take advantage of these opportunities. Failure to complete tasks that are rewarding despite his full ability to successfully complete them. He does not attract or reject people who treat him well. - He makes great and excessive sacrifices without asking the person intending to sacrifice for it - because sacrifice is a state of deprivation that he longs for, despite his claim that he is donates for other reasons.

However, none of the above cases is classified under general masochism if it occurs as a reaction or reaction to an excessive attack of Hamas, or when it is subjected to psychological, physical or sexual abuse or a state of depression.

Who is Masoch ??

Leopold von Sacher-Masoch was an Austrian writer and journalist born in 1836 in Galicia, which at the time was part of the Austrian Empire and Hungary - today divided between Poland and Ukraine - a province whose women are said to have a rare talent for adapting and taming their husbands !. The talent left an indelible mark on the memory of Masokh, who grew up in a wealthy family of Hispanic and Ukrainian noble origins.

Masoch studied law and history and is associated with literature, wrote many novels and stories, the most famous and most widespread of which may be the story of "Venus in a Fur Coat", which has been translated into many languages, and which tells the story of a man named Severin, who has an affair with a widow named Linda, and when the relationship between them surprises her with a strange request, as he begs, she should treat him like a slave, and encourages her to despise him and treat him humiliatingly. At first, Wendy takes this matter seriously, but gradually she finds it funny and rewarding, so she takes her role more seriously and gradually integrates with it, and at the same time, her contempt and contempt for Severin, who melts into a sensual and lustful pleasure increases with every blow and insult he receives. In the end, the relationship between them ends in the Italian city of Venice, where Wendy replaces him with another lover.

The story of "Venus in a Fur Coat" is taken from real facts. Her characters are the author of the story itself, that is, Mazuch, and his mistress, Baroness Fanny Pestor, psychiatrist Richard von Krafft-Ebing (Dr. Richard von Krafft-Ebing) is embarrassed to borrow the name Masoch to describe what later became known as masochism , in a book he published in 1886 on homosexuality, how what was written by Masoch was entitled to the most accurate and detailed literary effect in describing this type of anomaly.

That the tendencies of masochism of nationality are rooted in his childhood, and this may be the clearest imprint that characterized this childhood, is the memory of one of his relatives or aunts, Countess Zenobia (Xenobia (The Countess who occupied most of his imagination when she broke his heart his breathtaking beauty and the charm of his strong personality, which is why his heart was attached to this playful beauty when he was still a child of ten, and he especially enjoyed seeing her in the precious fur coats that filled her wardrobe. This love was nurtured. He grew up in his heart year after year, and in his masculinity, he felt an irresistible attraction to beautiful women who wear fur coats, as the walls of his house were overflowing with pictures of women in fur coats, and he begged his mistress to ask her to wear a fur coat, torturing him. Rather, a fur coat became a measure of a woman's beauty in Mazocz. If one of them liked it, he said about it: "I would like to see it in a fur coat. I those who did not like it, his face quickly turned away from him, saying: "I can't imagine seeing this in a fur coat!".

But let Mazoch's masculinity be put on hold for now, and let's go back to that ten-year-old boy who was flying with joy when his beloved Countess asked him for small favors, such as helping her wear her clothes when he felt elated when he grabbed her by foot to help her put the shoe in her little foot, And one day she didn't. The boy himself grabbed this ivory white leg by the chest and put a hot kiss on it. The Countess smiled slyly and realized what was happening in herself, and gently kicked him .. What a wonderful blow .. It had a magical effect on the boy, as if thousands of hidden wings lifted him into the sky and flooded him with waterfalls of happiness and ecstasy, which he never did not know.

But the most notable incident, which may have changed Mazoch's life forever, happened another time. One day, when the boy was playing hide and seek with his sisters, his legs inadvertently led him to the countess's bedroom to hide behind a shroud set in one of his corners. It is strange that the Countess returned home that day with one of her lovers, where she brought him straight to her bedroom, closed the door without them, then soon they threw them on one of the sofas and they exchanged hugs and kisses without feeling the boy's eyes. who peeked at them from behind the curtain. In fact, a boy Mazoch's age would not have seen such a scene, but if only it ended with this scene, what happened after that would be the most obvious and questionable .. It took only a few minutes until excitement rose, a screaming rose, and the door of the room She opened violently, showing behind him the countess's husband, a frowning face of anger, accompanied by two of his friends. It was a really awkward situation, the atmosphere of the room became fraught with fear and the eyes were looking at what the evil husband would do after he caught his wife dressed in crime, but to everyone's amazement, the Countess got up from her lover's arms and then Kurt fisted her and fell hard on her husband's face before he uttered a lip! .. It was an incredible sight when the evil husband was lying on the ground, and blood flowed profusely from his mouth. As for the Countess, it seemed like she went into a fit of insanity as she took the whip from the wall and started chasing everyone in the room with his painful bites, husband, his friends and lover !! .. Everyone ran away, do not twist on things, and unfortunately for Mazoch, she received one of the blows from the whip from the changing curtain, and she fell to the ground and opened his hiding place, and as soon as the eyes of the evil countess fell on him, until he hit and did not kick him without any mercy, the strange thing is that despite the force of the blows and the intensity of the pain, the boy felt a strange and hidden pleasure that seized his body with every blow !. Meanwhile, while Mazoch was receiving a harsh punishment, the countess's husband returned to the room, but he was not angry and mocked, like the last time, rather he seemed submissive and humiliated like a slave, he lay down at the countess's feet, begging to forgive him and forgive his sin! The Countess looked at him with contempt and kicked him again and again, and the boy found in her concern for her husband a great opportunity to escape, so he let his legs go to the wind and left the room.

But the boy didn't go far, after a few minutes of his escape, he felt a strange obsession, pushing him back into the room to see what was going on between the Countess and her husband, but this time his return collided with the closed door of the room, but the boy heard screams and the groans of the humiliated husband and the hum of the countess's whip, tearing the stillness of this place and violently hesitating Abdel. Door .. What a groan and the most beautiful cries! .. How the music looked sweet in the boy's ear .. How jealous the countess's husband was at that time! .. He wanted him to be in his place, receiving those painful, addictive and lustful whips at the same time !!.

The desires of the boy Mazoch and his abnormal imagination grew with him and later cast a shadow over his relationship with his mistresses and wives who endured his strange desires, sometimes because of jokes, sometimes because of experience, and because of resentment and blinks. But that did not stop some of them from really enjoying the experience, such as Baroness Fanny Pestor, who signed a contract with Mazuch in 1869, according to which she agreed that Masoch would become her slave within six months, she could torture, humiliate, and use it the way she wants during this period, but on condition that she wears - as much as possible - a fur coat when she wants his skin and torture !. Indeed, they went to Italy together, where no one knew them there, traveling on the same train, but the Baroness got into first-class cars, while Mazukh was happy to torture and humiliate himself, sitting in third-class cars. Masoch described his relationship and the facts of his trip with Fanny Bustor in his famous story "Venus in a Fur Coat," which we mentioned earlier.

In 1873, Masoch first married a young woman named Laura von Romelin, who also became a character in his stories. The beautiful wife soon discovered the strangeness and abnormality of her husband's behavior. One night, Masoch insisted that she whip him, but she couldn't do it and asked the maid to do this alien, who paradoxically had her last mission at Mazoch's house, as the wife saw that her survival became impossible after she hit over the head at home and was fired the next morning.

Laura gradually succumbed to her husband's desires, but reluctantly, she began to beat him with a long whip, which ends with sharp blades, and she began to suffer and insult during sexual relations, often in a fur coat, the poor never understood the fun and excitement that gripped her husband with every blow and with the insult that he receives, He tried to explain the topic to her, tell her that he needs to empty his abnormal desires so as not to master his thinking, and find time to think, write and write. But the problem is that these crazy desires were not limited to whipping and torture, as he was seized with a strange desire to force his wife to betray him! He begged her to take a lover, he wanted more torture! Psychological torture this time, perhaps to restore memories of the boy and the countess of flirting. The funny thing is that Masoch himself placed an advertisement in the newspaper to find a man who had a relationship with his wife! And when this man was finally found, he made an appointment with her at a city hotel; Laura went down there to pray and plead Mazoch, but when she met the man in the hotel room, she told him about her husband's behavior and fully explained it to him, so the latter refused to touch her and returned her home.

But the failure of the experiment was not late for Masoch, as he continued his attempts until he finally got a lover for his wife, and it is strange that he gave her up when she left the house to meet her lover, telling her: "How am I to him That is, he is jealous of his lover to have sex with his wife. Of course, as an inevitable end, Laura despised and despised her husband and turned her love for him into overwhelming hatred. Ironically, Laura finally fell in love with the lover her husband had prepared for her, so she left Masoch and went to live with her lover in Paris, and then the couple divorced in 1883 after a ten-year marriage and one girl.

Later in his life, Masoch married another woman, his secretary Hilda, and lived with her until the end of her life, Hilda coexisted .. Or rather, she found a way to live with the strange desires of her husband, and their marriage ended with the birth of two children.

There are some sources that claimed that masochistic intelligence had receded in recent years and that he died in a mental hospital in 1893.

In general, despite the natural swelling of Mazoch's actions, we must mention in conclusion that the man, as described by his wives and women who were in relationships with him, was a lover and an understanding and compassionate husband who does not drink, smoke and love his children. ... He was a kind and natural man when he was outside the bedroom, and even there Masoch never harmed any woman, but he liked to receive pain from them. Additionally, Masoch was an intellectual, great writer and fighter who participated in some of the revolutions and wars that devastated his era, and above all he was a defender of human rights and a fighter for non-discrimination against minorities; And I remember this conversation at the end of the biography and translation of this person for an important purpose, because I want you to understand which one is Honorable Reader, that a psychopath is like a physical patient, this is a disorder in his body, and this is a disorder in his soul , and this disease does not require contempt and mockery, but rather requires diagnosis and treatment. Not necessarily that a psychopath is a bad person, for example, what was accepted was a good person for most of his life, but he suffered from problems and does not suffer ?! Isn't life a journey of suffering? In fact, the person was mentally ill at a time when people knew nothing about the reality of mental illness .. Not to mention the diagnosis and treatment.

What are the causes of masochism?

As with most cases of homosexuality, there is no integrated theory or consensus about the causes of masochism, as the masochist may have had problems and personality disorders ingrained in his childhood, as we saw in Masoch's biography.

There are those who believe that masochism arises from the suppression of strange and abnormal thoughts and fantasies, because a person's constant attempt to suppress these ideas generates a strong desire to put them into practice, and if that person feels excited and enthusiastic about the application, he will associated with this desire and will continue to use it.

Another point of view argues that sadistic and masochistic practices are a type of escape practiced by some to reincarnate characters that are radically different from their true personalities.

Is it possible to cure masochism?

Behavioral therapy is commonly used to treat homosexuality, such as masochism, and this can include organizing and controlling arousal patterns, and developing and enhancing the patient's social skills.

In some critical cases, which can lead to significant self-harm or present a real danger to life, as in the case of hypoxiphilia, drugs and medical sedatives are used to control the patient simulation.

Masochism needs long and difficult treatment, just like the rest of homosexuality, but due to the social strangeness of the situation, most of the injured are ashamed to disclose their sexual orientation, and for this they suggest turning to a psychiatrist to get the necessary advice and help.

Is masochism a danger to others?

In general, a masochist, unlike a sadist, receives pain and does not direct it to others, but the risk is that he can seriously harm himself. For example, several deaths are reported annually in the United States of America due to serious masochistic practices.

PRISONER BEHIND BODY BARS

Over the years I have seen many films, Arab and foreign, in which women play the role of men, often in a laughing comedy dress. In real life, the country is almost devoid of "registered" women for many reasons, such as sexual dysfunction and homosexuality, including those related to freedoms and restrictions for women. But whether in the movies or in real life, it has always been easy to distinguish women, no matter how exaggerated and diligent they may be in portraying the role of men, except for a few who play the role with all their wounds until it gets difficult, even for women. , to distinguish them from men, and the heroine of our story of this type, Fatal succeeded in reincarnation. Her role is that she even married a man twice, and she lived for several years as a loving husband and a respected head of the family !.

With the advent of the second half of the nineteenth century, Europe witnessed a massive migration movement to the new world, millions of Europeans were overwhelmed with ships crossing the oceans to bring them to America and Australia to escape extreme poverty and chronic hunger, whole families sold their lands and homes, and donated precious and precious ones in the hope of a better life in the diaspora. The Valini Italian family was one of those poor European families who left their home in southern Italy to find themselves in New Zealand in 1877.

As with most immigrants, rosy dreams and high hopes for quick wealth and a comfortable life quickly evaporate and dissipate under the weight of hard work and low wages offered by their new homeland, especially since most of these unfortunate migrants lack common sense in planning. and managing their lives and financial resources, and this is true entirely in the Valini family, which worsened her position, the head of the family and his forbidden protector enjoyed an open and constant appetite for having children, apparently decided to have two dozen children, but fate and failure helped them with only 22 children! Four of them have died and seventeen remain open. Mr. Valini has to constantly feed her with his simple work as a rite of horses, and because this task seemed almost impossible.That is why Valini made his young children work to help him get more money, his eldest daughter Eugenia was not excluded from this (Eugenia Falleni) She wore boys' clothes and made them work hard jobs that were not suitable for girls. Thus, Eugene printed from the softness of her nails the nature of boys and drank their behavior. She soon left home at an early age while wearing boys' clothes, and then left New Zealand after getting a job on a commercial boat.

According to a novel that Eugenia told herself, her fellow sailors discovered the fact that she was a girl on a cruise and they took her to Newcastle Beach in Australia in 1898 and left her there when she was pregnant and it is not known how Evgeniya gave birth to her child, did the sailors rape her after they revealed her secret? Or was she in a relationship with someone on deck? In any case, her pregnancy led to the birth of her daughter Josephine, and because Eugenia had neither the psychological nor the physical qualifications to take care of the girl, so she left her in the custody of an Italian woman in the city of Sydney and left her again disguised as men. and this time she took on the character of a Scottish man named (Harry Liu Crawford). But Evgenia did not completely abandon her child while the child grew year after year, her mother constantly visited her and calmed her from time to time, then she later took her to live with her, and

Josephine learned about her mother's truth, but treated her before people as father and father.

Eugene, or rather Harry, worked in various jobs, in the meat market .. At the bar .. At the rubber factory .. Finally, as a driver and equestrian groomer for a doctor in North Sydney, and thanks to his work, his relationship with the director of the doctor's house for whom he works were strengthened, she was a lovely thirty-five year old widow named Annie. Burkett had one thirteen-year-old son. Harry and Annie have become loved ones! Harry claimed to his beloved that he was a thirty-eight-year-old widow living alone with his daughter Josephine.

In 1913, Harry Crawford married Annie Burkett in an official church ceremony and moved into the family home with his children. It is unknown when Annie learned the truth of her husband, but by 1917 it became clear that she perfectly understood that her life partner was only a woman like her, and since then the couple's relationship became tense, Annie began to threaten her husband to reveal their truth to everyone, the neighbors said that the couple's quarrels And their screams became He hears in the neighborhood almost every night, and in the end Annie completely disappeared and was never seen again, no one knows where she went, but Harry claimed that she left him and sent her son to live with his aunt.

A few months after Annie disappeared, the police found the body of a mutilated and burned woman in a park outside the city, and it will take the police a long time to identify the dead.

Harry soon married in 1919, this time to a spinster named Elizabeth King Allison, but their life together lasted only one year. The police identified the body that they found in the park two years ago, her son found out, in fact it was not only Annie Birkat, the wife of the Missing woman who suddenly disappeared in 1917, and having established that I started the police with suspicion of her husband Harry, all the evidence was that he lured her on the day of the accident to take a walk outside the city and then surprised her with his back and hit her in the head with a stone before he set her body on fire and left the place.

The authorities finally arrested Harry in 1920 for the murder of his wife Annie Burkett, and at the police station Harry's secret was revealed for the first time in years, they wanted to put him in a men's prison, so he asked them to put him in a women's prison and tell them the truth about him field, and it was really a surprise Incredible men The police are stunned. Soon the details of the case were released to the press, so her people and her correspondents began to delve into the past of Harry Crawford, and after a few days, only everyone in Sydney began to talk about a woman who lived a man and got married twice! It was an incredible story that angered many especially men who saw a scratch on their dignity! Moreover, the police found between Harry's men's clothes in his house similar male genitals made of wood and rubber, fastened with a leather belt, which led to the belief that Evgenia was a homosexual, the lesbian is deceiving women and awaits them in her cords, and this created a general feeling of hostility towards her during her trial.

The funny thing is that Elizabeth's second wife Harry was shocked when she found out the truth about her husband and bluntly told the neighbors: "Now only she knows why Harry was so shy ..." !!.

Evgeniya wore men's clothes at the first trial, but she came back and appeared in women's clothes in the second lesson, and she pleaded not guilty to the murder of Annie Burkett, but the judges found her guilty and sentenced her to death, then reduced her sentence to life imprisonment.

In 1931, Eugenia Valini was released after ten years in prison, and again she changed her name, this time she decided to become "Jane Ford", she lived in the suburbs of Sydney, where she ran a small hostel until 1938 when she was hit by a high-speed car, and the next day she died of her wounds.

Masud or Masuda?

The story of Yevgenia Valeni reminded me of a story similar to an Iraqi singer who lived in the first half of the last century, people introduced him to the name Masud al-Amartli - in relation to the Iraqi city of Amara - but in fact it was only a woman named Masuda. who was born in the Iraqi part of Al-Kahla in 1898 and lived to be an ordinary girl. age Eight ten.

Masuda tended the sheep in her youth for one of the sheikhs, she was a slender brunette whom God loved with a beautiful voice, and she praised the songs that she remembered during her shepherd's time, and one day she was waiting for two young people who were determined to be exposed to her badly so she bravely confronted them and then tied them with ropes and returned with them to the house you are working with, where two young people admit their guilt and admit that it was the voice of Masuda al-Shuji that seduced them by being exposed to it. The incident fostered a widespread reputation among the people, praising her courage and daring, encouraging and taking off women's clothing and wearing a cloak and mind as a man, which was not easy to accept in tribal society that women were lying in their lower gendarmerie, but Masuda imposed her presence on male councils with their spam and has become known since then in the name of Masoud Al-Ammartli, who became famous and achieved his reputation in Baghdad, recorded several lyric discs there.

One of the similarities between the stories of Australian Eugenia and Masuda al-Iraqi is that the latter also married a woman. Some accounts say that Masud was once a guest of Prince Muhammara when he saw and admired a girl named Kamla, so he asked her to marry and was associated with her, and it is said that Kamel Dest poisoned Masud and killed him when I found out that he is also a woman, while another story says that Masood al-Ammartli did not kill his wife or die poisoned, but he died in 1944 after tuberculosis.

The story of Massoud Al-Ammartli, whose events were reviewed by an Iraqi TV series shown in the nineties of the last century, in which the Iraqi singer Saadoun Jaber embodied the role of Masood Al-Ammartli.

Third floor

For women, reminding men is not news or is limited to our current era. For centuries, there have been women who have chosen to live like men, some of whom have spent their entire lives not knowing the truth about their gender, and this phenomenon is not always associated with homosexuality and homosexuality, as some believe, but its cause is sometimes so-called problems (Sexual Identity Disorder (Gender Identity Disorder) Where a man - man or woman - feels that he is living in the "wrong" body, all his feelings and feelings are of the opposite sex, but he is inevitable or forced to live his entire life in the chamber of his unaffiliated body. This problem has become possible to treat it today with the help of glandular and hormonal medicine and genital surgery, but in the days of Eugene Valeni and Masudatliya, a person with this disorder had to silently adapt to their suffering and suffer a lot of harm and torture.

Personally, I remember that during our high school there were many students who behave like girls who were subjected to a lot of harm and ridicule, one of whom I was a student in my class was a smart young man with masculine beauties, full of beards and mustache, but he spoke and acted like a woman. At that time, we did not understand that it was not in his hands, but that he was out of his control, but understanding his condition was not something that concerned us as much as ridicule, so we got to know the society .. Not to understand and not to pardon.

Understanding the suffering of people with sexual identity disorder does not necessarily mean accepting the deception and lies of some of these people, especially those who have undergone complete sexual transformation (Transsexual) These people should clearly disclose the truth about their gender before entering into a relationship of love or marriage with anyone human. On the contrary, the case can have serious consequences. As the saying goes, the rope of lies is short, that is, as happened with Eugenia Valini when Annie Birkat did not tell the truth about her gender before marriage.

MIRACLES OF LOVE ..
FEMALE TEACHERS!

Some time ago, I read a story on one of the sites about the trial of a teacher who had a sexual relationship with one of her minor students, and because I am the type of ram who does not rest until he surrounds all aspects of the story, so I kept looking and look for more information .. I wish I hadn't .. What I found shocked me, because the problem of this teacher was not only one of dozens, but hundreds of similar problems that arose in different schools around the world during the last few years .. Some have even compared the epidemic! .. The calamity is that we are used to being men who are always the heroes of rape and sexual harassment, but women do it with this number, and in this dastardly picture it is amazing !. And the great catastrophe is that they are teachers, some of them are married and mothers, and those who lack goodness and beauty to hunt adult men, what happened to them and what happened to them? .. Is it a mental illness? .. Or is it emotional deficits and sexual libido? .. Or is it love .. And the heart, and what he likes.

This may be the story of American teacher Mary Kay Liturno (Mary Kay Letourneau) And her brown student, Philly Fualao, is the most famous of all the teacher stories, but it can be considered a story that has drawn people's attention to the existence of such abnormal relationships in schools, and this served as a wake-up call to reduce this sexual abuse of teenage students. Here, some may object to the last phrase, that is, to view this issue as a crime of a teenage student who may seek to enter into such a relationship, and in which he finds what adults find in sexual contact, we were all students, and not it was odd that we were emotionally or sexually attracted to some of our teachers.This fact cannot be denied that there is nothing wrong with mentioning this because these feelings are unwittingly fueled by the explosive instincts of the adolescent body. There is nothing wrong with these feelings if they do not go beyond imagination and delusion, but the problem, when it turns into reality and action, it has been scientifically proven, dear reader, that sexual relations of a teenager and emotional attachment to an elderly person can have destructive negative consequences for his life in the future, and he has a lot of exploitation because his feelings are inexperienced with the life and nature of society, emotional and sexual relationships, and for this reason, legislators in most countries of the world began to protect the student from such relationships by passing laws to guarantee that he is not subject to sexual exploitation, harassment and rape by adults.

Returning to Master Mary Kay's story, this beautiful wife and affectionate mother of four suddenly passed out and whispered in love to one of her students in her primary school teaching practice, a brown Polynesian student named Fili Fualau, who was then twelve years old.

At first, Steve, Mary Kay's husband, did not negotiate his wife's close relationship with his student, but doubts began to sleep with the man when he saw her that the boy was paying more attention than her four children, so she brought him home after school. and did not leave her even during the summer holidays, until His presence became the cause of frequent quarrels and quarrels between spouses, these quarrels slowly increased until they found a response from neighbors and relatives who whispered and flattered about the nature of the relationship between the teacher and her student.

In the end, Mary Kay was forced to end all this confusion about the relationship with the boy, she had no other choice, she was pregnant and she knew that her brown skin birth would reveal her hidden secret, so she clearly confessed to her husband during one of the quarrels that the fetus in her intestines is not from his crucifixion, rather he is the child of Philly boy. In response to this bold confession, the husband called the police, telling them about the sexual relationship that his wife has with her minor student, and this relationship is punishable by law, since one of her parties did not come of age.

During preliminary investigations, the student confessed to the police that his relationship with the teacher began when he was a student in her class, and that this relationship first took the form of compassion and care, and then suddenly turned into a relationship of love and love, it happened one night when his teacher took him to his home as usual after spending most of the day at her house. As every time, a warm goodbye kiss was printed on his cheek, but the kiss that night unwittingly turned into an intimate exchange of kisses and hugs, then drew him to his rear car seat, where they had sex for the first time, and since then they have been hundreds of times, often in her house and on her husband's bed, while her children play in the next room

Mary Kay herself did not deny her relationship with the boy and received a reduced sentence of six months in prison, since she was fired from school. She was then released in 1998 after signing a pledge not to approach Philly again, but she obviously couldn't get away from him for long. She was arrested just a few weeks later while having sex with him in the back seat of her car parked on the street and so her case exploded again, But this time with a lot of media momentum and she was traumatized by American public opinion like Mary Kay was not an ordinary woman, she was a thirty-five-year-old adult woman, teacher, nanny, married woman and mother of four older children whose lover is a year younger! On top of all this, her father was a former member of Congress and a former candidate for the US presidential election in 1973 year. Due to these combined issues, her sentence was harsh this time around as she was charged with harassment and sexual abuse of a minor and sentenced to seven and a half years in prison. While in prison, Mary Kay divorced her husband Steve and gave birth to her second child with her lover Philly. She was freed again in 2004, and after her release, covenants of love renewed between her and her beloved Philly, who is now a 21-year-old young man, and they stole the light again in 2005 when they got married at a small party attended by the group relatives and friends, and they are said to now live happily with their children, despite the large age difference between them.

The funny thing is that one of the journalists recently asked Mary Kay, who is now a grandmother, if she agreed that her 13-year-old daughter would have a sexual relationship with her teacher at school, as it was between her and her student. Mary Kay replied categorically, explaining that girls are sexually different from boys, in other words, a teacher has the right to have sex with his student, but the teacher has no right to do the same with his student.

The student kidnapped the teacher!

26-year-old American teacher Angela Comer was more extreme in her love for her teenage student than her colleague Mary Kay, as this beautiful young woman abandoned her husband and left everything behind .. Home, family and work .. Flee to Mexico with his lover after taking her five-year-old son with autism. The lover was fourteen years old and his reckless teacher took him in his car to Mexico to marry him, far from the rule of American law, which prevents her from marrying him because she is already married and that he has not yet reached the age of majority.

The two lovers shared a room in a Mexico City hotel, stayed there for two weeks, but in the end they failed to fulfill their dream of marriage. The minor pupil required the consent of his parents to be able to marry under Mexican law, which was not available to him as his parents did not know anything about his place, which prompted them in the end to inform the police to solve the mystery of his sudden disappearance ...

The curtain was lowered in the last chapter of the story of the two lovers when they were arrested outside a Mexican police checkpoint and they were immediately transferred to the United States, where the student was returned to his family without revealing his name to protect him from defamation and Invasion by journalists, and Angela's child was returned. The patient was brought back into the arms of his father, Angela, in a lengthy trial that lasted sixteen months. The funny thing about her case is that she tried to avoid her crime by claiming that she was a victim, that a teenage student kidnapped her and forced her to drive thousands of kilometers to Mexico at gunpoint, and that she tried to escape from him several times. but he caught her every time, Even when he once smashed a guitar car on her head !. Of course, these accusations did not concern anyone. This adorable kidnapper and broken monster was only a fourteen year old boy, as he can do it all. Thus, nullifying her arguments and exposing her lies, the young beauty found herself in a lonely solitary cell to spend ten long and boring years behind her cold bars.

Eccentric teacher

The epidemic of female teachers was not limited to the United States, as this emotional stress spread to other parts of the world. In Japan, teacher Noriko Shimomura, 43, fled with one of her teenage students, despite being a married woman and the mother of three children, the oldest of whom is her lover.

Shimomura, a music teacher at a high school in Tokyo, spent several nights accompanied by her sixteen-year-old teenage boyfriend in hotels and small dormitories, and no one noticed how the teacher falsely claimed that her little lover was her son and that they were going on a trip to country and it is unlikely that they will be arrested. If not for the message that Shimomura's husband passed on to the police to reveal the fate of his wife five days after her mysterious disappearance. Shimomura later admitted to the police that her relationship with the student had taken on an emotional and sexual character from about a year in one of her classes, and said that she didn't matter after graduating from high school, so she decided to run away with him.

Shimomura's schoolgirls spoke to reporters after her case exploded and they called their teacher an eccentric, saying that she makes students feel her belly and chest under the pretext of teaching them how to control their muscles while singing. According to Japanese television, the "forbidden relationship" between teacher and student ended with the student returning to his family safe, while the teacher continued his face towards jail, as Japanese law punishes sexual relations with a minor in prison and a financial fine.

Thirsty teacher of love

N.R. - 26-year-old Muslim teacher, married and teaching in high school in New Zealand (1), veiled, but takes off her hijab at school. Her case exploded in 2008 when one of her students in class revealed the secret of an intimate relationship with him, the boy was fifteen years old and he bragged about having sex with the teacher several times, and mocked her masochistic tendencies, so he said that she asked him pinch her nipple hard, insult and treat her like a sex slave. He also claimed that she rewarded him for this relationship by letting him cheat on the exam, but at the same time, she threatened him with failure if he told anyone about their infamous secret.

The news of the teacher-student relationship reached the school administration through some of the students, and soon the police who had arrested NR were informed of the accusation of having sex with a minor. During the trial, N.R. admitted that she was attracted to the boy when he was a student in one of her classes, that they exchanged love songs and messages on the phone, and that they met and met several times at night in her car, but denied having had sex with him. But the proof and proof were all against the teacher. The letters of exchange between them were sexual in nature, as the student's parents testified that the teacher came to their house and took their son into her car, and that he sneaked through his room window several times without their knowledge to go with him. As for the student himself, he testified before the judge that his teacher took him at night in his car to one of the empty positions to have sex with him, and that they had sex once in his bedroom while his parents were out.

During the last session of her trial, "NR" expressed her remorse and shame for her actions and justified this with her growing up and strict upbringing, which played a large role in isolation from colleagues at school and university. She did not know love and did not have emotional or sexual relationships with men before marriage, until her marriage was emotionless, because it was arranged by her family and this emotional deprivation made her yearn for any real love relationship, and so she quickly succumbed to her student when he sent her a love letter over the phone on Valentine's Day.

The judge sentenced HP to two years in prison with suspended execution and to work for several hundred hours in the public good, and some objected to this punishment as being very diminished compared to the harsh punishments received by other teachers who did the same. most, but the court justified its reduced decision by psychological harm, stress and ostracism. The society that affected the accused because of her religious and ethnic background, in addition to losing her job and preventing teaching for the rest of her life and including her name on lists of sexual harassment , "NR" was ostracized by her family, husband, friends and relatives and ended up alone in a government shelter, and this is something that has more punishment than imprisonment in his brutality and isolation.

"She oiled up" her daughter's lover

American teacher Michelle McCatian, 38, surpassed her female counterparts in terms of deterioration and vulgarity, she not only took a teenage lover among the schoolchildren she works for, but went further, so she decided to have this lover as her only daughter's lover, and she recorded her sexual relationship with him on photographer tape. Unfortunately for her, it was this tape that ended up signing her as her teenage lover showed it to his friends and he also showed off nude photos of the teacher that she collected for herself and then sent it to her cell phone. This tape and photographs led to McCathian being suspended and arrested by the police.

McCathian admitted that she had sex with a student several times, one of them at home, and also admitted that she was sending her nude photos to her cell phone. But her business did not end there. Police investigations later uncovered other sexual relationships that brought her along with other teenagers, some of whom were students in her school. To make matters worse, finding a pornographic tape in her apartment during which she appears to have sex with one of the students in front of her only fifteen year old daughter, then forces her daughter to have sex with the same boy and she takes pictures and guides her during practice .. What a respectable family !.

A teacher or a prostitute ?!

I find no suitable description for American teacher Abe Jane Swagger, 34, other than her description of a prostitute, and I don't think there is any insult to her in that description as she already worked as a dancer in a club tonight before she became a teacher, or rather the help of a teacher, and she obviously longed for her old career, despite her retirement. Dancing and her vocational training, so I made sure to give free private lessons in immorality and immorality to her dear students !. But she did not do this in her house for fear of exposing her case among the neighbors, rather rented a small apartment for this "highly educational" purpose, and she equipped this apartment with a lot of perfume, drugs and condoms, and also brought two teenage girls. who ran away from home to help her serve the guests of her crazy party. She named him Many of her students at school, some of whom were friends of her only fifteen year old son.

During the ceremony, the al-Fadilah master completely passed out .. That is if she already has an iota of mind and feelings .. I had sex with everyone .. Boys and girls .. She ended her crazy party by providing a "technical" link which highlights her old talents, so she danced and undressed with the students and let them take a picture of her while she was naked, and this was her biggest mistake as these photos were not distributed to the students and transferred them by mobile phones while she was the news did not reach the school administration, which rushed to inform the police, who in turn threw Teacher under arrest for sex, alcohol and drugs for teenagers. The charges against Abe Swagger amounted to 40 charges, most of which were dropped in exchange for an agreement between the prosecutor's office and the accused, which requires her to plead guilty to a judge in exchange for reducing her sentence to 3-6 years only after her the expected sentence was 36 years in prison. Swagger's last words before being sent to prison were: "I wish I was the role model I was supposed to be."

The teacher loved his student

The case of British teacher Helen Goddard, 26, sparked interest in the press and people for the poetic relationship that brought the young teacher and her fifteen-year-old student together. Although society did not accept such an attitude, most people sympathized with the blonde music teacher, she was not homosexual and she had a lot from men in love, she was a talented and skillful musician, playing the trumpet to the point that she was called "Lady of Jazz". and above all she was kind-hearted and loved by everyone, especially her students, who are very attached to her, some of them did not leave her even during the break between classes. The principal warned her not to strengthen her relationship with her students more than the acceptable limit, to tell her that additional friendship with a student can have negative results and it seems that the person's intuition was in order.Helen's relationship with one of her students gradually developed from an innocent chatting and drinking several cups of coffee together in a cafe near the school, to a burning love affair during which they shared a bed together for five months.

The teacher and student communicated with each other to such an extent that they exchanged messages of love and love, and the student spent every Sunday evening in his teacher's apartment without the knowledge of the parents, she falsely told them that she had spent the night at the house of one of her colleagues, and One day, two lovers went to France together for a week to take part in an Annual Gay demonstration while the girl's parents thought she was going on a school trip to the countryside. But the rope of lies is short. In the end, everyone learned about the relationship due to the student's slight tongue slip when she brought one of her colleagues to steal her close relationship with the teacher, and so the news spread and spread until he heard the student's parents who filed a complaint with the police against the teacher.

Elena did not deny her relationship with the student, she directly admitted to the police that they had sex for the last five months, but she insisted that what unites her with the girl is love in the first place, she loves the girl very much and will not stop her love, whatever the consequences, and the girl, in turn, told the police and her parents that she loved her teacher And that she would continue to love her forever, and before this love and mutual wandering, the judge raised the state of the amateur teacher and sentenced her to only fifteen months 'imprisonment, and he rejected the student's parents' application that the teacher should not contact his daughter for five years. This affair ruined Helen's future as her name was on the sexual harassment register and she could not teach for the rest of her life, but Elena remained true to her love and showed no remorse. She told reporters who cried when she was sent to prison that the first thing she will do when she is released from prison is "Call your sweetheart."

Husband killed his lover

The adventures of sex teachers are often risky .. scandal, exile, divorce and imprisonment .. Sometimes it can lead to death, as happened in the case of the master Irene McClain, 30, who had sexual relations with one of her students and continued in these relationship to such an extent that she brought her lover to her home and had sex with him with her two sons, 11 and 8 years old.

The story began when Irene met student Sean Boyle, 18, a student at her school.At first, Eren felt sorry for Sean because of his painful childhood because his mother was a drug addict and was adopted by another family, but this sympathy gradually turned into a mutual feeling of love In exchange, Irene's relationship with her young husband, Eric McClain, was going through the most critical time, and Eric found himself in a difficult psychological situation due to his preoccupation with studying and work at the same time, he sought to complete his studies at the university and at the same time work for two positions in the morning and evening to create reasons for a decent life for his wife and two children, and his constant preoccupation with this led to the fact that the relationship between him and his wife was cool, who began to talk to him during that period about her student Sean, and about his harsh conditions, Eric sympathized with the student to such an extent that he welcomed him to his home and worked hard to find an alternative for him. after his adoptive parents kicked him out of his house for drug use.

Eric thought his wife's relationship with a student was innocent, motivated by kindness and compassion, but doubts began with the man when his wife spent long hours every day talking to Sean on the phone and he would sometimes come back from work and find him at his house. and his doubts about his wife's betrayal were confirmed when his eldest son told him one day that Sean accompanied them on a walk in a public park, and that his mother and Sean were holding hands like lovers and kissing.

Irene denied her betrayal and she played an innocent role with a lot of ingenuity that made Eric regret blaming her, but a few days later, Eric returned from work to find Sean at home with his wife, so he asked him to leave, but Sean refused to leave. so Eric called the police and asked them to come to get Sean out of his house.And then Irene intervened and asked Sean to leave the house, he did it at her request, but he soon came back and stopped his car in front of the house, and then started screaming with Eric that he would take his wife away from him, and Irene had already started to collect clothes to leave with him, but before she could leave, Eric went outside after seeing his gun and asked Sean to leave the house immediately, but Sean refused this do and nervously pulled Eric's hand out, trying to pull the pistol out of his hand, and an accidental shot that settled in his head and killed him instantly.

His trial, Eric McClain, received a lot of media attention and everyone sympathized with him as a cheated husband. His sentence was reduced by just two years in prison, given that he didn't intentionally kill Sean. As for Irene McLean, she took her children and fled to another city where she took a pseudonym and started teaching at a charity school, but she soon lost her job after my father filed a complaint against her, accusing her of sexually harassing their son. and she not only lost her job because of this complaint, but lost the nursery. She also has a favor for her husband and the two boys have moved to live with their grandparents awaiting their father's release. In conclusion, teacher Irene McLean was not prosecuted due to her relationship with Sean because he was eighteen years old when she had sex with him, and Irene later claimed that her relationship with the student was with her husband's knowledge that their marriage was broken off even before she met Sean, and that there was an agreement between them that their marriage was open, that is, they remain married only to humans, and they continue to live under the same roof for the sake of their children, but each of them has the right to take a boyfriend or lover, and the other does not mind it. But Eric completely and in detail denied these allegations during the trial and said that his wife used his difficult psychological state during this period to manipulate him.

The lover killed her husband

Contrary to Irene McLean's case, the roles were reversed in the case of American teacher Pamela Smart, this time the student was the murderer and the husband was the victim, and this issue received a lot of attention in the American media for its disgrace and low motivation.

The story began in 1988 when Pamela Smart took a job as a teacher and media coordinator at a high school in New Hampshire, where she met a student named William Flynn, 15, and their relationship gradually developed into love and sex. The student was attached to his teacher to the extreme, and she completely controlled his mind and feelings, as it was the first love in his life, and the first woman to have sex with her, and he was ready to do anything for her, and she I took advantage of this affection and blackmailed him in the worst way, because she threatened him to end his relationship with him if He did not save her from her husband, I told him that she would be alone and would marry him if he killed her husband. On the evening of May 1, 1990, Flynn stormed his teacher's house, with a pistol, and hid there with one of his friends, awaiting the return of Gregory Smart, WHO, as soon as he entered the house, attacked him and shot him in the head, not caring about his requests to save his life. Late at night, Pamela Smart called the police, screaming and sobbing, and told them that she had just returned home to find her husband drowned in a pool of blood.

Immediately, the police launched extensive investigations to uncover the mystery of the crime, and quickly discovered the sexual relationship that unites Pamela Smart and her student Flynn, then investigators managed to catch Pamela through one of the students she had with her, and Blaine was friends, so they put a voice in her clothes and made her lure Pamela even in conversation. She told her bluntly that it was she who prompted Flynn to kill her husband and was motivated by this in order to obtain the value of his life insurance policy of forty thousand dollars.

Police arrested Pamela Smart and her lover, William Flynn, and they were put on trial for first-degree murder. This case ended with Pamela Smart being sentenced to life imprisonment for (9999) years without any option for amnesty, and Flynn was sentenced to 28 years in prison. Pamela Smart has been brutally beaten over and over again by her colleagues in jail and has claimed that she was stalked and raped, and her nude photos were leaked from the jail, and her pardon request was rejected multiple times and she recently told the media that she prefers to execute what he meets from the dark days inside the prison.

What exactly is going on?

These questions, which he wrote about in this article, are just an example. A researcher of stories about sexual relations between female teachers and students can find dozens of them, which may require mentioning and detailing a full book, and I can almost assure that these issues in general represent only the apparent head of the mountain. God knows how many of these relationships occur every day around the world and go unnoticed without being discovered or aware of them. The bewilderment in this huge spiral of stories and problems lies in the motivation that can get a respectable adult teacher to have sex with her teenage student .. The rationale that allows a married woman in her thirties, like teacher Jennifer Rice, to kidnap her student under ten years to have sex with him, or it makes a teacher named Annie appear at the doctor. Phil's program (Dr. Phil) recognizes to millions of viewers that the real father of her two children is her fifteen-year-old brown student !.

Researchers give a thousand reasons and justifications for sexual relations between teacher and student .. As a psychological state .. And a troubled marriage .. And a lack of emotion .. And the desire to try something new .. so on .. But the secret of the steady growth of these problems remains difficult puzzle to solve .. What exactly is going on? .. This is an epidemic .. Or is it a love of imitation .. Or that these things have happened in the past, but we have not heard of them due to the lack of modern means of communication such as the Internet, satellite and mobile, and if so, what is the true number students who have been raped throughout history by male and female teachers .. Does this happen in our schools, or is it limited to schools in the West? .. I personally think this is a common case.

Before imprisonment .. In order not to be accused of prejudice, men are the heroes of undeniable sexual harassment, and their harassment is often more painful and painful for a child than a woman's harassment, just as men are willing to pursue their whims to the fullest. For example, we rarely heard of a mother who raped her children, I personally heard about this only in one case, cases of rape by parents of their daughters and sons became so numerous that parents began to be afraid to kiss their daughters in public, so that they would not be accused of pursuit !.

Finally, we must remember that these problems that we have mentioned here are only individual, rare and abnormal occurrences. Most of our teachers and teachers are wonderful people who hold a high and great place in our hearts. We will continue to respect them throughout our lives, just as their fragrant memories will be renewed in our minds and consciences whenever we meet them by chance. At the corner of the street or at the corner of the market .. so on ..

WOMEN RAPE MEN

It is known that the accusation of sexual harassment and rape is closely related to a tenth of men since the time of history, and in fact this is not an accusation, but a reality that a person has practiced from the time of the cave before that. day. Greed for booty and women has been at the forefront of temptations and incentives for men to accompany invasions and military campaigns. Nowadays, when the police and the law are in force, it is, of course, difficult to kidnap and rape a woman in broad daylight, so a man can whisper and touch as a form of compensation for the past "glories" of the past! And pour out his pent-up sexual desires. Of course, we are not talking about all men here. Some of them - just a few - are persecutors or rapists. On the other hand, a woman is also a person whom God loved with feelings and lust, but, thank God, Eve's thinking is very different from Adam's thinking .. A grown-up natural man may not mind having sex with any available woman .. Sometimes even with a bloody, old , obese, etc. For him, the problem is simply emptying lust. As for women, they are not sexually attracted to men equally, they are not ready to have sex with any man, except for money. In the natural state, passion and admiration must keep pace with lust so that a woman can give her body access to pleasure and ecstasy. In addition to passion and a way of thinking, the measure of physical strength, and the nature of the formation of genitals is not in the interests of a woman, so it is rare to hear about a woman who raped a man, yes, she can bother him, and she can seduce him with her sweet talk and seduce her body, but she rarely seeks physical strength and violence to achieve the goals of nationality. It is for this reason that cases of rape of women among men are among the rarest and most subtle cases.

One of the strangest questions I've read in this area is the case of a Russian woman who was described by the press as a "black widow." This woman hit the wall with everything that we wrote above, because she was not satisfied with the rape of one man, but the number of her victims exceeded ten men!. She hunted them in bars and nightclubs, seduce them with her beauty and take them to her home to give them wine with a large dose of clonidine, and as soon as the man passes out until she begins to undress him from his clothes, and then begins have sex with him for hours while surrounding his penis with a strong rope to stay upright !. After she swiped her fly away from him, she dragged her victim to her car and then tossed it to an empty space away from her home. The police began to suspect this after several people arrived at the hospital with similar symptoms. Dizziness and dizziness with swollen genitals. The last thing all these men remember is to sit with a beautiful and beautiful woman. The police finally managed to contact the woman who seduced and raped men. It was a thirty-two-year-old woman who revealed only her name "Valeria. TO". The funny thing about this case is that one of the ten victims of Valeria refused to file a complaint against her, he just got angry because he did not mention anything that happened on the night of his rape. He told reporters sadly: "I liked what this beautiful woman did to me, but I wish she hadn't used clonidine with me." !. There is another funny case of rape of men by women. This time in Zimbabwe, where a gang of four young women raped men to get their cum !. I don't like the dear reader .. Sperm in Zimbabwe is very expensive, as a large and fresh package is sold for almost three hundred dollars !. It is for use in magical rituals of fertility and femininity. The gang usually encouraged men to go with them in the car, sometimes under the pretext of instructing them, and as soon as the victim gets up, he is forced to wear a condom at gunpoint, then they have sex with him and collect his sperm.

Many of the 17 men filed a complaint with the police, claiming that they had been raped by a gang. The police subsequently succeeded in arresting the gangster girls as a result of conspicuous stoning, with which they found a condom that they used to store semen from their victims. It is said that men in Zimbabwe today are very afraid of women and that men run on the run as soon as a woman's car passes. We stay in Africa to tell you the story of "Aruko Onoga" who was raped by his six wives !. Aruko was a wealthy, well-to-do man living in the province of Nigeria who was a follower of pagan religions that allowed polygamy without borders, and he was known for his extreme love for sex and women, so he was not happy with one wife, rather six wives. But he was unfair to them, he loved the little girl who spent most of her nights with her. And he continued this way until the revolution against him one night, when he returned to his house and went, as usual, to his younger wife's room. He almost lay on his bed until the rest of his wives burst into the room, armed with knives and sticks, they were angry and avenging the exclusivity of the young wife, so they forced him, at gunpoint, to have sex with all of them that night, from youngest to oldest !. Thus, Aruko continued to have sex with his wives one by one without interruption, and the man almost successfully completed his mission, but he felt very exhausted while living with his sixth and last wife, and he fell out of bed unconscious. The younger wife talked about what had happened, saying, "Suddenly my husband stopped breathing and the other wives left the room laughing. But when they saw that I could not wake him up again, they all ran away and disappeared into the forest. ". The men of the city were very saddened by Orko, who set an example for them in relations with women, as no, and he is the "resettlement" of the city, but what a loss .. "Fall" quickly fell during sex. Nigerian police have launched a hectic search in an attempt to find deadly wives.

SHE HAS HAD SEX WITH 1500 MEN .. SHE IS STILL AN HONORARY LADY!

Alternative sex is a type of behavioral therapy, as claimed by practitioners, whose purpose is to address patients' sexual problems through education, guidance and application-. Accordingly, treatment sessions involve teaching the patient through sexual contact, whispering and touching, up to practical application, that is, full sexual contact between patient and therapist, and for this reason most therapists are women and most patients are men. ,. More precisely, the alternate sex for a woman (convert) is to teach sex to a man on behalf of her wife or girlfriend. Or, a (processed) man teaches a woman the origins and art of sex on behalf of her husband or lover.

Okay, why do people resort to someone to find out something that they have by nature? ..

In fact, medical and psychological statistics show that a significant proportion of men and women have serious bedding problems .. Sexual weakness .. fear .. Shy .. Lack of self-confidence .. apathy .. Final speed, etc. Here why so many of them resort to medical and psychological treatments to overcome their sexual problems, and alternative sex is one of those modern treatments.

In the past, some men, if they wanted to learn sex, or overcome their fear and shame for sex, all they had to do was find an experienced prostitute, but today, like these people, they prefer to go to the Mir Simone clinic. which is one of the treatments that have worked in the field of Sex Alternative for 23 years, during which she has advised more than ten thousand people, and had sex with more than 1500 of them.

Miss Samouni's work differs from a bitch in the following way: firstly, she has experience in psychotherapy and behavior, Secondly, it does not cause embarrassment in men and is patient, kind and understanding, The third advantage is that her work is legally permissible. The last advantage is that she periodically undergoes a medical examination to study sexual ailments, and she does not have sex with her client until he comes to her with a health certificate confirming that he is free of any sexual ailments. As far as the similarities between her job and the bitch are concerned, she adds up to getting paid for sex and not wanting to sleep with any man.

Miss Simone is not ashamed of her job, it is true that she hides his nature from her family and relatives, but she considers herself a decent working woman and she loves her job and talks about it, saying, "I make my living sleeping with other husbands and loved ones. But I am by no means a prostitute, because alternative sex is a legitimate business, if it is practiced in the context of treatment, men push me to solve their sexual problems, and not for the sake of one sex. ".

Miss Simone is now in her fifth decade and has a large private clinic in America, which explains the nature of her work, saying: "There are those who become an alternative mother because she would like to help another woman have children, and this is how I work. to make the lives of other women happier and more vibrant in how to sexually educate your husbands and friends to be better partners in bed. ".

According to Ms. Simone, most men suffer from sexual problems, and many of them are not suited to make their partner happy with bedding, even to make themselves happy. This is the role of alternative sex therapy.

The therapy sessions begin with a regular conversation and conversation with Miss Simone holding the client's hand to give him more confidence and comfort, and in subsequent sessions, physical contact with the client increases, touching the shoulders, hips and buttocks, then the nudity stage begins, where Miss Simone is completely throws their clothes, and so does the patient.Then they stand in front of a large mirror and do different exercises, and the purpose of this stage is to increase the patient's confidence in their body, how many people are ashamed of their bodies, until the last stage, which on demand, involves sex between miss Simone and the patient, and usually requires access to these Stage 12 sessions, each session costs around £ 100.

According to Simone, she has helped many men gain self-confidence through treatment sessions, so their warm sex life has become brighter and more energetic, and for this many of them come to her clinic at the request of their wives and loved ones! ...

Of course, Miss Simone is not alone in her field. There are other treatments practicing the same profession around the world, and there are many stories and online interviews with them. Some of them are famous and have appeared in documentaries. Perhaps the most famous of them is Mrs. Sherrill Cohen Green, 68, says she has had sex with over nine hundred men for thirty-three years as a sexual treatment. Perhaps the strangest thing about Mrs. Sherrill's story is that she received her patients at home with her husband and children, and she had sex with them on her family bed in her bedroom! ...

Mrs. Sherrill's husband was one of her patients, he had erection problems and had no problem keeping his fiancée in her profession after the wedding, and he never objected to her sleeping with other men even after she became a mother and grandmother.

Mrs. Green earns $ 300 per session. She was recently very famous for a film based in part on her life and profession called Sessions, in which movie star Helen Hunt looks completely naked and plays a sex appeal that helps a disabled person.

Like Miss Simone, Mrs. Greene insists that the goal of her work is not sex, but to help men with sexual problems, a quarter of her male patients have never had sex in their lives out of fear or shame and helped them overcome it.

The number of sex therapists in the United States and Europe is not significant, perhaps because this profession still causes a lot of social and moral controversy, as most people consider it to be just convincing prostitution, as is the case with the so-called massage clinics (Massage) Where are beautiful girls massage the bodies of men, and their services often go beyond simple massage and sex.

But sex therapists like Simone and Green claim they are not prostitutes, despite having sex with hundreds of men. The strange thing is that most of them are married and have children, and according to some sources, most of those who work in this profession are the wives of psychiatrists. And they all insist that they are respected respected women who have done a great service to society by contributing to the life change of many of their patients, not only from men, but also from women, because the treatment of men's sexual problems benefits their partners in bed. their wives and friends, because of their sex life, plays an important role in the development and strengthening of bonds and relationships. Especially if we know that many divorces are caused by sexual apathy among husbands.

Of course, there are men and they have female clients, but the number of men in the profession is much lower than that of women, as we said earlier.

finally .. What do you think, dear reader, about alternative sex .. Is it an honorable profession for treatment and repair? .. Or is it just prostitution and convincing prostitution? ..

WHO LANDED FROM THE SKY .. HAVE SEX!

We have heard a lot about flying saucers, These mysterious spaceships come from distant worlds to visit us, Which comes and goes for an unknown reason and without bothering to notify us of its existence, Perhaps for this reason, It is, repeating the same the scenario is always, Which does not go beyond seeing something move and quickly disappear in the sky, Most people have lost interest in the topic, The stories of flying dishes are no longer as exciting and attractive as they were several decades ago, It became without taste or meaning, We never understood why flying dishwashers are trying to travel billions of miles through endless space to our planet, which is too trivial to see in the giant crowd of our Milky Way .. They overcome all this great distance to stand among the clouds in for a few moments, and the one-eyed farmer looks after his cows in the field, then they return to wash without rest and talk !! ...

I am personally bored with this nonsense, That's why I rarely write about it on my website, I want to hear something new, More than just mysterious lights and bodies fly fast in the sky, I hope to wake up one day and open the TV and see a flying saucer that landed on the square at the opposite end in London, on the red square in Moscow, or near the pyramids in Giza .. I see its passengers go out and talk to us humans, They tell us that we are not alone in this existence, They take our hand, They change our life and our perception of things, They teach us how to poison each other over our hatred and hatred, How to live in peace and happiness in a developed world, in which there are cures for every disease, How we stay young for centuries , We spend our summer vacations on Mars, We buy apartments and houses on the Moon, We exchange messages through the space "network" with friends and family on distant planets and galaxies.

What dream ! .. I don't think this will ever happen .. That's why let the world of dreams go away and return to earth to talk to you about some of the most unusual stories in the field of flying saucers, heroes of people who claimed to have passed more than just seeing lights running fast in the sky .. Much more ..

Hot brazilian evening

It was a magical night in 1957 .. The sky is clear, full of stars, and the night wind gently flirts with green spices, so the fields from afar look like a stormy sea face scattered across its page, isolated islands of hamat of tall trees. The whole existence was drowned in an enclosed silence, which was only disturbed by the noise of insects, the chirping of frogs, and the sound of an old tractor led by a young man named Antoino Vilas Poas who worked at night to avoid the high temperatures during the day.

The clock meant a quarter and one after midnight, when Antonio looked up and saw a red star shining strongly in the liver of the sky. The young man stopped his tractor and began to observe this star, asking himself what could be. When he was preoccupied with his ideas, this star began to grow in size and shine, as if it was falling to Earth at a supernatural speed. It took only a few minutes until he stood directly over Antonio's head! ... It was not a star, as he thought, but rather an oval body with a large dome on top and a bright red light shining from below. For a while, he stopped floating in the air, then three metal lists came out of him, and he began to land vertically until he carefully settled over the field .

The paranoid Antonio tried to escape, but the tractor stopped working for some unknown reason, so he jumped off and started running at full speed towards the houses near the field. But he did not go far, once he was surrounded by four people in uniforms somewhat similar to the one worn by astronauts, they caught him and then forcibly carried him to their mysterious oval boat.

Antonio described his captors as taller, each wearing a gray suit, and each suit has a circle on the chest that emits red light. They used to wear long high-heeled heels and wore huge helmets that covered the entire head, of which only two pale eyes looked blue. From each helmet, three tubes branch downward to connect to the uniform at three different locations, indicating that the helmet is hiding some kind of advanced device.

Inside the car, Antonio found himself in a room free of windows and furniture, with its walls shining as if it were daylight.Then his captors soon took him to a second room, similar to the first in every detail, except for the presence of a round table in in the middle, surrounded by several unsupported chairs, such as in bars, In this room, Antonio first heard his captors talking to each other, He was very surprised at the words of their words, Their language was like barking! …

After they spoke a little - or, rather, barked - the kidnappers stripped Antonio of his clothes, then sprayed him with a strange substance with the power of a gel and took him to a third room with vague marks on his door. In this room, they took a sample of his blood with a device that they inserted into his chin without feeling pain. Then they went out and left him alone.

Antonio was wrapped around him, the room completely empty save for a large bed floating in the air with no pillows or pillows or covers. Antonio sat down on this bed and soon accepted his thoughts and concerns, wondering what fate awaits him at the hands of these strangers. Soon, he suddenly felt tight in his chest and saw white smoke flowing through the fine pores in the walls, feeling nauseous and vomiting in the corner of the room. Then this smoke quickly dissipated, and the door of the room opened again to enter the cosmic being .. Surprisingly, this creature resembled women of the earth .. And completely naked! ...

Her skin was light white, her eyes were wide blue, her mouth was small with thin lips, her nose was normal and straight, and her hair was light and white. As for her height, she was as short as the residence of her colleagues with a uniform, and the most beautiful of her body, as she convinced the perfect strength, and it was complete without wastefulness and accumulation, minute waist, thin neck, with enchantment envious the kindness of cinema. In fact, this cosmic gland differed from human women only in its small tapered chin and red hair under the armpit and on the pubis.

The cosmic woman entered the room, looking at Antonio with a view whose significance was not lost ... The look while he saw it in the eyes of the women who had sex with them, Realize quickly what you want, His fear and turmoil left him completely after as she stood in front of him and brought her naked body closer to him, He found in himself an irresistible attraction to this global beauty, He grabbed her hand and gently pulled her to sleep, He unexpectedly found it with him as a guide, With jing and pamper . It denotes groans and voices of pleasure and ecstasy. At the same time, he found in himself a strange power to continue and renew, so he lived it over and over again relentlessly, even if one of those uniformed aliens didn't enter the room after an hour .. Maybe he never stopped! ...

Having entered the alien, Hasna got out of bed and was interested in going out with her colleague, but she turned to Antonio before leaving with a smile on her face, then wiped her stomach with her hand, pointed at him and nodded towards the sky. Antonio realized that she was telling him that she would take his child to live with her on her planet. Realizing that the purpose of his entire abduction was to have sex with this space .. Perhaps the aliens wanted to improve their offspring, so they chose a human stallion for this purpose, and Antonio felt very pleased with this conclusion, feeling a little pride and shame for that what was the desired stallion! ...

Antonio was left alone for some time after Hasna left the space, and then two of the uniforms entered him, so they returned his clothes and took him back to that room, which was mediated by the table, where four of them were sitting on a vague language as if they were in a meeting. It was obvious that they had lost interest in Antonio, He seized the opportunity of their concern and began to reflect on what was around him, He looked at the little clock cube at the end of the room, He told him to take it with him as proof of the veracity of his abduction, But as soon as he grabbed this cube, someone stood up and gently grabbed it and then put it back.

The aliens took Antonio on a tour of their boat. After the tour ended, someone accompanied him near the car and left him in the same place from where he was first taken, Then the alien returned to the car, which soon began to rise vertically in the air until he reached a certain height, with bright lights painted from the bottom of the car, and then set off like lightning to disappear into the liver of the sky in an instant.

Antonio stood alone, amazed, near his tractor. He looked at his watch and found that it was pointing to the fifth, which meant that he had spent nearly four hours in that car. He set up his tractor and locked himself home.

At first, no one believed Antonio's story of his abduction by aliens, who laughed at his friends, believing that he had imagined it all. But a few weeks after his abduction, Antonio developed strange symptoms .. Headache .. Nausea .. Convulsions .. Blisters and spots on the skin .. Doctors were confused by his diagnosis. But when he told them his story with aliens, some of them suspected that this was the cause of his illness, he could be exposed to the substance or high doses of radiation. A committee of intelligence officials, doctors and atomic scientists is said to have researched Antonio's story and in fact discovered high levels of radiation at the site where the spacecraft supposedly landed. Thus, Antonio's story became exciting news reported by Brazilian newspapers and newspapers, and people were divided into two parts about this, some believed it, while others saw only illusions and hallucinations in his story.

Due to disagreements over his history, Antonio was a man of great honesty on the part of his friends and acquaintances. He later graduated from college in his life, worked as a lawyer and died at an early age in 1991, leaving behind a wife and four children.

Sleep with the lizard boy

Many people are afraid of lizards, They don't want to approach her or even just touch her, And for those, The idea of sex with a lizard seems terrifying and ridiculous, But it is not so for American Pamela Stonebrook.This blonde jazz singer claims to have shared a bed with a lizard, And that her experience was wonderful in every sense of the word! .. To be honest, Pamela is not talking about an earthly lizard here, but about a 6-foot space object that looks like a lizard, and about her experience that says:

"The first time I had sex with an alien was different from all the love jokes I've known in my life, it was interesting and fun, and without going into details, I can say that it was more than most men. whom I knew. Just remember how it felt when I first saw it, I woke up from a dream and found myself having sex with a Greek god, At first I thought I was dreaming, But the sex seemed very realistic and intimate, When I closed my eyes, I was amazed at the comfort which I find in the hands of this object, Then when I opened my eyes again and found that this Greek god had turned into lizards with scaly skin like snakes, Then I realized that I was having sex with an alien who is able to switch from one form to the other, when the subject saw the features of panic on my face, it whispered in my ear, saying, "We've always been together, we love each other." I felt very enthusiastic right away. "

But this romantic experience with a lizard was not actually Pamela's first encounter with aliens, as her knowledge of them dates back to 1994, and that first encounter she says:

"At that time my work was long and tiring, One night, I went home and went to bed early, But instead of getting up early and going to work as usual, I woke up from a dream to be inside what looked like a cosmic a ship, I was hanging like a fruit inside a severed and dim pyramid, She looked nervously around and found a row of small gray creatures walking around the room and looking at me. One of these beings, and I think she was a woman, addressed me with the words: "Don't be afraid .. Just come with me. ".. I followed her into another room and closed the door behind us, and as soon as we went outside the door, this object disappeared, I saw three other creatures, but they were smaller and feminine, and she shouted to me, saying:" Mom . ". I was very anxious and I saw myself in my bed again. This experience made me scared because it looked very realistic, and when

I washed my face and lifted my sleeves, I saw little scars on my hands, so I began to return the details of my experience and remembered that these creatures had caught me from the same place, and this explains the appearance of scars. I couldn't sleep well that night, in fact I slept poorly for almost a year. ".

To get rid of the terrible obsession that night and find out the truth about what happened to her, Pamela came to the hypnosis sessions, and about this she says: "It was wonderful because he brought back a lot of memories, which convinced me that I had many encounters with these aliens. It was amazing because I saw the idea of having other worlds as a very ludicrous idea, but I started looking at things differently after my experience. I even asked an artist to paint my impressions of this alien and created a group to support people who had similar experiences. It was difficult at first to tell my parents and friends about my story, but I quickly got over the factors of embarrassment, and I honestly don't care if people laugh at my story because I was like them before I met these aliens. ".

Chinese farmer and space giant

"She was three meters long and had six fingers in each hand, and her hair covered her legs, except that she looked like women." This is how the Chinese farmer Ming Chogua describes the cosmic creature with whom he allegedly engaged sex.

The story began in 1994 when Ming and two of his relatives were working in the field and turned their attention to a metal object falling in the forest at the foot of a mountain adjacent to the field, so Ming thought it was a hovercraft or hot air balloon and went to find out ... When he reached the crash site of the metal body, he was surprised that what he thought was a hovercraft that carried people aboard, but they were gigantic and powerful. Min entered the flying saucer and stayed with these creatures for a while, and then returned home.

On the evening of the same day, the cosmic creature pursued him to his home, where they had sex for forty minutes while they floated in the air of his bedroom, while his wife and daughter slept in bed below them. This space left a small scar on Ming's thigh, which I later see for reporters, confirming the truth of his story.

A few weeks later, the aliens returned again and took Min to his car, but this time he did not see his owner of the space, and when he asked them about it and asked to see it, they told him that it was currently impossible, and they told him that in sixty years the child will be born from a crucifixion on another planet.

Min claimed that the aliens took him with their car on a tour of Jupiter, And that he saw the Earth from space with a crystal ball, He saw damage to forests, glaciers and lakes due to human pollution, The aliens told him that humans must do something do to quickly save the environment, or the Earth will die.

Ming's story is the most famous in China in the field of flying saucers, and Ming is said to have passed false tests, and these tests proved to be true of most of what he says.

Space rape

At two o'clock after a cold and dark night in 1973, Mrs. Gabriela Versace was driving her car alone on the highway near the English city of Longford Budville, returning home after visiting a sick friend in another city. The road was completely empty except for dim light, and distant Gabriela thought it was from the car before her, But it seemed steady without moving, When she approached him, it quickly flared up and gradually weakened until it was completely extinguished, Like as soon as the light disappeared, the engine of Gabriela's car began to cause a strange fuss, and then completely stopped for an unknown reason; Gabriela was very scared, Like not when she is a lonely lady, standing in the dark, on the street without a man at this late hour of the night. She got out of the car, opened the front cover, and then stared desperately at the engine, As she tried in vain to find the source of the holidays, He heard a faint hum, Then the sound began to increase and gradually approached, But he did not find its source, Suddenly, she felt a strong hand landing on her shoulder, Then she found herself on the floor, When I turned to see the attacker's face, I was surprised by the long metal body, like a robot standing on it, then everything sank into your darkness.

When the light came back again, Gabriela was in a grassy field, There were no tracks of her car or highway , Next to her, this mysterious robot stood, Right in front of her, she saw a huge metal body emitting a bright light, It was in the shape of a hemisphere 12 meters in diameter and six meters high, Above him are many rectangular windows, Below this, several huge metal sheets appeared to support him in his standing. Gabriela's stay in front of this enlightening body did not last long, as everything again quickly drowned in darkness.

When Gabriela opened her eyes again, she was in a very cold round room, and next to her was the robot that had kidnapped her, but now he is standing motionless.

Gabriella was lying on a metal table and she was completely naked, but she was covered with a blue blanket and her arms and legs were tied to the ends of the table.

After a while, three men entered the room with moderate stature and slender bodies, wearing hoods that cover their heads and wearing masks that hide their mouths and noses, so that only their eyes look like human eyes, but they look more round and look hard without feeling.

Three men ran a suite of tests on Mrs. Gabriela with devices and machines that she had never seen in her life, and they took samples of her hair, blood and nails. During these trials, one of them did not say a word, but from time to time they looked at each other and shook their heads as if they were talking to each other by telepathy. But when someone saw Gabriela looking at a standing robot without movement, he spoke to her in English and told her that this robot is a programmed device to work outside the mother ship, its main job is to bring samples from abroad for study and study. Then the three men left, and Gabriela was left alone in the room.

A few minutes later, one of those people returned alone to the room, went down the table, took off Gabriela's cap, and then stood looking at her body, Gabriela felt that something terrible was going to happen, She turned to the table, trying to free herself in vain, When the man saw her excitement and panic, he took a small pin out of his pocket and stitched it into her thigh, and her whole body went numb except her head and she stopped moving completely.Then the man slowly climbed to the back of the table and lay down over Gabriela and he slowly raped her without moving his body! .. Gabriella described her feeling at that moment as uncomfortable, but did not feel pain, and after the man finished this, he got up from the table and left the room.

After a few minutes, the three men returned and freed Gabriela from her chains, then took her off the table, and when she looked at the floor, she found her clothes at her feet, and then everything sank into darkness again.

When Gabriela opened her eyes again, she found herself wearing full clothes and standing next to her car at the edge of the road. She went to the car and turned the key. To her surprise, the car started working immediately and she drove her back to her home in a deplorable state of shock and horror.

Gabriela told her husband what happened to her, They agreed to leave the story to themselves and not tell anyone, But think about what happened and curiosity to know more about these mysterious people, All of this ultimately prompted Gabriela to turn to experts and specialists in the field of flying saucers for advice, The world was thus introduced to the details of its strange history.

Queen Pussy Sex!

One morning in June 2013, Mr. Simon Parks took the world off the screen of the fourth English documentary to launch a heavy bomb, This fifty-two, And a member of the British Labor Party, He claimed to have had sexual relations with aliens since he was six! ...

Mr. Parks showed viewers a painting depicting the first cosmic creature he had ever known, claiming that the first meeting between them took place in his childhood, and that this creature was: "Green seven feet long and in a pink robe." And the creature took Mr. Parks with him to his spaceship as follows: "We held each other's hands, then I say I'm ready, and then we immediately moved to his spaceship orbiting the planet with technology I can't understand."

Mr. Parks claimed that he had a long-term relationship with a space creature named Queen Pussycat, and that they met four times a year to have sex. Not only that, the cosmic creature got pregnant from mister. Parks and gave birth to a child named Zarka.

The broadcaster asked mister. Parks, saying, "How can a six-year-old have sex?" Mr. Parks replied that the problem was different for the aliens, as their gender cared more about the soul than the body.

As for the impact of his cosmic romance on his family, especially when he is a married man with three children, Mr. Parks says: "My wife knew about this and was unhappy, it gave me some problems. But my relationship with aliens is not human, so I do not feel guilty or see anything wrong with what I do. ".

MEN'S HOLIDAY

For some men - and I am not talking about all men - the penis is the most important, most expensive, higher, and future member of any other organ member, surpassing its importance even in the brain, and I am not exaggerating when I say that there are people who never do not think through his mind, rather it is the center of thinking And his intellect is stable and limited by his testicle ... Otherwise, Lord, does it make sense for a man to rape his daughter or sister or attack a small child - accidents that occur daily in different parts of the world - does someone with a little mind do this ??! ...

But it is also fair to say that not all men wander in love for their penis, there are those who take revenge against him for hating him, because he continues to push them to life, poisoning their thoughts and multiplying their sins with his endless desires and whims, so you will find that one of them sits in the safety of God while he is in a wonderful state of highness, serenity and spiritual purity .. And suddenly, without ideas, the terrible head looks like a cursed demon to destroy and disturb this wonderful moment. Unsurprisingly, you will find someone muttering angrily, "I wish I could cut him up and get rid of him." ... And really ... There are those who cut it and get rid of it. Thousands of castrations occur annually around the world.

One such operation was a young Japanese hero named Mao Sugiyama - 22 years old - who has a rare condition known as nationality (asexual) This lack of any sexual orientation or desire, despite the fact that the reproductive system is complete and does not suffer from any defects, and this situation occurs in men and women by one percent, and for people with this disease - or grace - the penis is considered an excess and useless member! ...

Our friend Mao decided to get rid of his cock, so he went to the hospital and underwent surgery to destroy it, and a few days later he returned to his house carrying his male cock cut in a frozen container and upon arriving at the house, hellish the idea came to mind that there was no "donkey" before. "Another on the face of the globe. The idea is to cook and eat your penis, according to the saying:" The first offense with the flesh of his revolution. "..

But before Mao put his penis in the pot, a new idea came to his mind, which was more hellish than the first .. He decided to offer his penis for sale on the Internet, so he posted his tweet on his Twitter account, saying, "I offering you a delicious meal consisting of my penis - complete with testicles - for only one hundred thousand yen ($ 800).) .. By the way, I'm Japanese

He wrote in another tweet: "The organ was surgically removed when I was 22 years old and I went through full and accurate tests to make sure it was free of sexually transmitted diseases. For your information, the participant was working fine and was not using female hormones. ".

He also wrote: "The first buyer interested in an offer will receive a full participant. I don't mind selling this to the group. It will be cooked to the taste of the customer and at the location of his choice, and if you have any questions, please contact my email. ".

Of course, dear reader might think that nobody has applied for a male member .. But let me surprise you .. Suggestions poured onto him! ... It sold out quickly and it was decided that there would be a big party to take it to the ballroom in Tokyo, and seventy people attended the party as well as reporters, but only five people ate the dick for $ 160 each ... These five are a thirty-year-old couple, a twenty-second young woman, a man in his thirties and a 29-year-old party organizer.

Mao forced the buyers to sign a document, according to which they will be responsible for everything that happens to them after eating a member.

The organ was then presented as a soup with mushrooms and parsley, and it was eaten completely.

A journalist asked buyers about the taste of the cock they were eating and said it was very rubbery and almost tasteless.

It's worth noting that Mao is now planning to sell his nipples! ...

What do you think of this story, dear reader? .. You could say that Mao and those who ate his penis are a bunch of assholes .. But let me give you the stupidest thing .. This time our hero is an African young man from Malawi named Jamangani Zulu. The charlatan and impostor convinced this poor guy that he must present his penis to a hyena in order to get rich! ..

God, have you ever heard a recipe like this ?? !! ..

And because mister. Zolo was ready to do everything to get rich, he went into the desert and willingly stood before the hyenas .. Such a generous person! .. And good luck for the hyenas .. I can confirm that it was the easiest food they ever had ..

Mr. Zolo's wait did not last long as one of the hyenas soon came and began to destroy his body .. You can imagine the scene, dear reader .. The hyena is devastated by this poor man's flesh as he stands motionless, endures pain and leaves in a dream of wealth. which will soon befall him .. This is a dream from which he woke up in the hospital only after he lost three fingers from his hand in addition to his penis.

Of course, this poor guy is not to blame, as he is a naive and simple person due to the ignorance of Africa, but what are we talking about a genius computer engineer who presented his whole body to be eaten willingly .. It was the German brand Brands that responded to the ad. written by its citizen Armin Meves, which said: "It takes a strong man between the ages of 18 and 30 to kill and eat." ..

Meaves took Brenda into his house and he filmed his murder and cut it all out on TV and it started with Brands' penis, after Meefs gave a lot of painkillers and drugs to brands, he tried to cut his cock with his teeth but couldn't so he brought a knife and cut it, then he took it to the kitchen, put it in a saucepan and added salt, pepper and some garlic for it, then he came back and presented it to Brands to eat it together, but the latter became weak and weak from - for bleeding and could not eat his penis, so Myths took him to the bathroom and left him bleeding for a while, and then came back and killed him. He peeled the skin off and then put the meat in the refrigerator and continued to eat it for several months.

LOVE STORIES .. IT ENDED IN TRAGEDY

Perhaps the most common stories that people have spread in their councils and forums, and whose reputation has flew away until perspective is applied in their glory, are those that speak of love, so there is hardly a myth or old folk tale about mentioning devotees biographies lovers who struggle with hardships and risk their lives in order to reach their beloved and receive his satisfaction. It is good that most of these stories end with the lover reaching his goal, where we see him meet and marry his beloved, to live together in "pat and plant" for the rest of his life and in untold happiness. But unlike those fictional folk stories that grandmothers told on cold winter evenings, reality and history .. They say something else. Love, like other things, is subject to weakness, withering and loss, and its enemies are many, so many great love stories end in tragic tragedies, and this is exactly what we will tell you in our article .. Famous love stories that ended in sorrow, catastrophes and great disappointments.

Cleopatra and Antony

Cleopatra was the last ruler of Egypt from the Hermitian family, a family of Macedonian descent taken from Alexandria as the capital of its king in the third century BC and the city became a beacon of science, literature and art. Ptolema was fully integrated with Egyptian culture, traditions and religion to the point that some consider them to be an extension of the Egyptian pharaohs.

Cleopatra crowned the queen of the year 51 BC. with her husband - her younger brother - Ptolemy XIII. But she fled Egypt after the differences between her and her husband became clear, then she later returned and crowned the queen again, this time as the wife of her other brother, Ptolemy XIV, with the help of Julius Caesar, who became her lover. It is said that she seduced Caesar with a clever trick, sneaked into his palace wrapped in a rug, and when they extended the rug in front of Caesar, Cleopatra came out of it as if it were a nymph who robbed his mind and immediately stole his heart

After the assassination of Caesar in Rome, Cleopatra became the mistress of Mark Antony, who was one of the poles of the alliance, who took on the task of revenge on Caesar's assassins, but this union did not last long, as the war began between his poles, Antony and Octavius, and this war ended in battle at Actium, where Antony was trapped near Alexandria after losing his fleet and escaping from his army, there was false news of Cleopatra's death, so he decided to commit suicide and implanted a sword in his stomach, but he did not die immediately as he did was transferred to Cleopatra's palace and took a breath and he died there between her arms, moans and tears, then she also committed suicide, said she hugged an Egyptian cobra snake, was bitten and poisoned, and her bridesmaids are said to have committed suicide in the same way. With her death, the reign of unemployment in Egypt, which became the Roman state, ended.

It is unknown if Cleopatra committed suicide with sadness over Antony, or because she knew that the new conqueror, Octavius, was not tempting and that he intended to roam her naked on the streets of Rome before sacrificing her in the Temple of the God Jupiter. ... Unfortunately, this is the humiliation experienced by another eastern queen, Zenobia or Zeba .. But that's another story.

Cleopatra gave birth to three children by Antony and one by Caesar, while her marriage to her brothers went nowhere, indicating that it was a formal marriage, nothing more.

Octavius, later known as Emperor Augustus, was the first Roman emperor after the Republic. He later killed Cleopatra's son by Caesar, fearing that he would fight him for the throne of Rome.

Cleopatra's name was not erased by her death as it became an icon of beauty, cunning and female seduction, written by many, including William Shakespeare in his famous play Cleopatra and Antony. Her life has also become the material for many films. The strange thing is that the sculptures, inscriptions and coins that have fallen into the hands of archaeologists about Cleopatra do not show them the beauty described in the novels and films.

Duchi's mistress

Clara Petachi was born in Rome in 1912, her father was a private doctor for the pope. Due to the softness of her nails, only one man, Benito Mussolini, was in Palais and Clara's heart. It was a strange kind of love ... A young girl loves a married man who is twenty-eight years older than her, and what kind of man? .. The fascist dictator of Italy, the man who took responsibility for the revival of the glory of ancient Rome.

At the age of fourteen, Clara sent an emotional message to Ducha congratulating him on escaping the assassination attempt. Mussolini admired this message, so he ordered his secretary to write a response to the girl and thank her, which increased his admiration and Clara, attached to him. Years later, Clara was walking with her fiancé when Duci accidentally drove through his car, this was the first time he saw him on earth and his vision of her heartache changed, chasing the dictator on the streets of Rome and flooding his office with hot love letters ... How happy she was when they called her and said that Duchy had agreed to see her.

Many may not know that Mussolini was a womanizer. According to Clara herself in her diary, Duchy was addicted to sex. His office manager once said that one of his responsibilities was to prepare a dozen women daily for Duci to choose three or four wakes with him. There was a private sofa in Doci's office while he had sex with his female visitors, some of whom were high-profile and famous, and it was even rumored that he was in a relationship with the Queen of Italy.

Now imagine, dear reader, a minister of women like mussolini, a beautiful young woman comes in and introduces herself to him like Clara, what will be his reaction? .. The answer is on the couch, of course! ... From that day on, Klara became Duchy's official mistress, of course, she was not the only one who shared his bed, there are others, but Klara was different from everyone else, because Duchi really loved her. The relationship between them was fiery, raging, epic, as she detailed in her diary, in contrast to Doochy's relationship with his wife and mother of his four children, Rachel, who was cold.

The relationship with Duci returned to Clara and her family with many benefits, she had her own palace, which had a swimming pool, tennis court and bomb shelter, but her days of happiness did not last long. The war began and the whole world saw Mussolini lined up with Hitler, then he fell with him whenever the winds of victory changed towards the Allies. From the fourth year of the war, the Allies captured the Italian colonies in Abyssinia and Libya, and Rome itself was threatened with collapse.

The story of Mussolini's life and rise and fall need long pages to explain, but what worries us is his final chapters. After the Allies occupied Italy and moved north, Duci and Klara tried to escape to Austria with a column of defeated German soldiers, but the convoy fell into the hands of the anti-Italian resistance movement behind Mussolini, Duci, who was hiding in the back of a truck, was arrested, and Klara was with him, like her brother, who tried to escape, and they killed him.

Mussolini, Clara and their companions were taken to a farm near the city of Dongo, and out of fear of human resistance that Mussolini would be saved, they rushed to execute him, killing him at dawn on April 28, 1945. It is said that they chose Klara between staying or leaving, so she decided to stay and die with her lover Duchi. It is also said that the last sentence Duchy said before his death was directed at his killers, where he shouted at them, saying, "Pay straight to your heart."

After their murder, the bodies of Mussolini and Clara were taken to Milan and hung upside down in a public square. Thousands of people gathered to see the bodies and threw rotten shoes and vegetables on them, and Mussolini's body was presented.

Clara was taken out of bed to death without even being able to wear her underwear, so when they hung her upside down her skirt fell off and her nakedness was exposed, people condemned it and some of them covered it up by wrapping her skirt around her feet as shown in the picture.

The bodies remained suspended for several hours until the Allied soldiers arrived, so they dropped them off and were buried in an unknown grave.

In the 1950s, Ducha's tomb was excavated, Mussolini's remains were transferred to his family's cemetery in Predapio, and Clara's remains were buried in her family's graves in Rome.

Shah Jahan and Mumtaz Mahal

Prince Khurram, Crown Prince of the Mughal Empire in India, was a handsome young man who had girls' hearts blowing, but his heart fell on only one girl, the love of his life ... Great store.

He was fifteen when he first saw her at a party, she was a year younger and he was in love at first sight.

After preaching for five years, the two lovers were married in 1612. On the contrary to most love stories, the young prince's love for his beloved did not disappear after the wedding, but rather an increased flash and glow, especially after he discovered the tenderness of her creation and the predominance of her mind, since she did not interfere in state affairs and did not participate in intrigues and intrigue, like most court women. And due to the seriousness of the prince's affection for his wife, he took her with him wherever he came and traveled, even in his travels and wars, no wonder he had fourteen children! ...

In 1628, Prince Khurram ascended the throne of the empire after the death of his father, he became known as Sultan Shah Jahan, which means king of the world. His early years of rule were accompanied by some unrest and revolutions, and some governors revolted.

The sultan himself set out in 1631 to subdue the governor of one of the Afghan rebel provinces and, as usual, he took his beloved wife with him, but it seems that the long and arduous journey has exhausted Mumtaz Mahal, who was pregnant at the time, and her the birth was difficult, and she was about to die, so the sultan rushed to her and sat in her head, shedding tears, and it is said that Mumtaz Mahal She looked at him before she died and asked him about two things. Firstly, never marry her, so that she does not have other children who are fighting with their children, the Sultan, and secondly, build a unique shrine for her in order to perpetuate her memory forever. The Sultan approved two requests and he remained tied to her head in the hope that she would recover, but soon she sighed and turned to her innocence, and it is said that the Sultan retreated after her death for a whole year, and when he went out to the people again, his hair was completely white and his back was bowed.

The Sultan fulfilled his covenant with his wife, and after that he never married and built for her a burial temple, which the world had never seen in splendor and beauty. This Taj Mahal, or marble poem as he calls the Indians, is a verse of architecture and the wonder of the wonders of eternity, and under its unique dome, the two lovers meet again as it includes the tomb of Mumtaz Mahal and her husband the Sultan, who was buried next to her. after his death .

Bonnie and Clyde

Sometimes people admire and sympathize with criminals and criminals, Froben Hood and Ora Bin Al-Ward were only Chinese and bandits, but people loved their biography because they stole from the rich to feed the poor. Don Corleone was a dangerous gang leader in The Godfather, but people loved him so much that some of the suggestions he made in the film were out of the question! .... Bonnie and Clyde were two murderers whose hands were stained with the blood of many, but in the end they turned into a legend that lived in the conscience and memory of many people.

Clyde Barrow was born in 1909 near Dallas, the fifth of seven children. The extreme poverty of his family prompted him to steal at an early age. Most Americans were poor during the Great Depression. In 1930, Clyde was arrested for theft and sent to the infamous Estheim Prison.

Clyde was a handsome young man who was sexually harassed by the rest of the inmates, and there, in prison, he committed his first murder when one of his rapists was beaten to death.

Something was broken in Clyde and could no longer be repaired, his sister Maria says: "Something terrible must have happened to him because he was no longer the same person when he got out of prison."

They became the only Clyde, and the axis on which his life revolves is to take revenge on the regime. He wanted to punish those who caused his imprisonment and rape, so he began to kill and steal without mercy or relentlessness, not until the theft itself, but to revenge on the part of the security personnel, who, naturally, became the majority of his victims.

Bonnie Parker, born 1910 in Texas, her father died as a child and lived with her mother on the outskirts of Dallas, she was very distinguished in school, won awards in spelling, rules and public speaking, and gave poetry. Unfortunately, she dropped out of school after marrying one of her 16-year-old colleagues. It was not a successful marriage, as the young couple split in 1929, but they never formally divorced, and when Bonnie died years later, the engagement ring was still in her finger.

Bonnie came back to live with her mother after the separation and worked as a waitress, and by chance I first met Clyde at a friend's house, so they immediately admired each other, and soon Bonnie became Clyde's mistress and a key person in his gang, accompanying them and participating in stealing banks, shops and gas stations. Bonnie rose to prominence after newspapers published some of her photographs with a Cuban cigar in her mouth and holding a pistol in her hand, so that this stereotype of her as a rebel girl is printed in the minds of people, although her gang colleagues later said, that she hadn't actually smoked a cigar or killed anyone herself. But Clyde did, he and his numerous colleagues, most of whom were from the police, were killed, and he managed to storm the Estham prison and free some of the prisoners, which no one had done before or after him ... All of this made the authorities declare him "an enemy of the people, "and a large financial reward was awarded against his head and Bonnie's.

One day, Clyde kidnapped a man and later freed him without harming him while he was in the car with the gang. Bonnie asked him about her profession and said he was a shop, so Bonnie laughed and said that one day she could work on her body.

In 1934, Clyde and Bonnie were killed in an ambush as they drove their car down a bleak outer road near Louisiana, dozens of bullets were emptied into their bodies.

Thousands of people gathered for the lovers' funeral. Some offer to bury them together, as Bonnie wanted, but her family refused. I don't need to tell you, dear reader, who took over the delivery and disposal of Bonnie and Clyde's body .... This is the same store that Bonnie was expecting to bury! ...

Bonnie and Clyde became legendary in the myths of love and crime. Unfortunately, we cannot take note of the details of their history in this rush, but dozens of novels, films and TV series have talked about them over the years. Perhaps the best thing we conclude with our words about them is that Bonnie ended her poem "The End of the Road," where she says:

One day they fall together, they bury them side by side for a few. It will be a police grant, it will be a relief, but it will be death for Bonnie and Clyde.

THE STRANGEST STORIES OF LOVE AND MARRIAGE

Love is beautiful, there is no doubt about it, but not all love is beautiful, as there are types that seem mysterious and abnormal to the point that people stop there when they are empty of mouth, either from the seriousness of the surprise, or because they are going vomit with the severity of disgust. There are, for example, men and women who love to kiss their beloved feet and feel their tongue, and there are people who feel delighted when their lover curses them, hits them and spits in their faces! ... Of course, you can say that these things are a form of homosexuality and have nothing to do with love and love, but I personally see them as a form of love. What is love? .. Is it not the attraction of something and extreme attachment to it, what we call a person, attached to a doll to the extent of flirting, kissing and relaxing in bed .. Is it love or anomaly? .. I consider it love, but it is a strange and unacceptable love for others who have overcome this love only between a man and a woman. In this article, I will show you examples of love that lacks logic.

Marrying dogs eliminates bad luck

If you are unlucky, marry a dog .. This is proven Indian wisdom! ..

In 2007, the media reported on Mr. Silvakamur (33) is a stray dog, and their wedding took place in a remote village in India with about 200 guests.

Okay, why did he marry a bitch .. Are women extinct in his village? .. no .. mr. Silvacamor's marriage to a dog was not caused by the absence of women, but by a bad deed that he committed twenty years ago. As a teenager, he stalked and harmed animals. He once killed two dogs with stones, and after he killed them, he hung their bodies from a tree ..

Since then, Jinx has been following Mr. Silvacamor as punishment for his disgusting act against two dogs, and he says: "After killing two menstruating dogs, my legs and arms were paralyzed and I lost my hearing in one of my ears."

The village magician told him that the only way to push the evil eye was to atone for his guilt against the dog, and that was only by marrying the dog. Indeed, mister. Silvacamor took the advice, and his choice was made on a stray dog that was found wandering the streets of his village in search of food waste, so he took her to his home and married her after several days of a noisy party attended by his friends, relatives and some journalists.

The funny thing is that the bride got bored during the wedding, she looked around and said to herself: "Damn .. What brought me to this crazy village? ".. Then she let go of her legs, she escaped from the wedding, so the audience chased her until they caught her and brought her to the groom who tried to court her and persuade her to stay with a little milk and a few bones.

Human marriage to dogs is not unique to India. In another case, a young Indian woman, Mangli Munda (18 years old), married a stray dog and the wedding took place in the presence of relatives and neighbors.

The Mangly family believed that their daughter had a curse or charm that caused her unhappiness, and that her marriage in this case would lead to disaster, most likely her future husband would quickly die after her marriage to him. To remove this curse, Mangli's father went to the elders of the village for advice and help, and he advised him to marry her with a dog because it would end the curse and change her luck for the better.

Mingli's father searched for a dog suitable for his daughter in the ruins and debris until she was found. Soon the wedding ceremony took place, it was not a fake ceremony .. No .. Rather, real ceremonies, such as those that take place at any wedding between a couple of people and the girl's family, were generously spent on this event. One of the conditions for lifting the curse is that the wedding must be realistic, but, of course, it does not have the same sanctity as a real marriage, because the bride has the right to marry later on a person of people.

Mingli told reporters that she is not happy to marry a dog, but she was forced to live a happy life.

"The village elders told us that we should have the wedding as soon as possible. We have to make sure the curse is broken and marrying the dog is the only way to do this. ".. Mingli said.

According to local journalists, weddings like this are occasionally held in that remote area of India where ignorance and poverty are high, people there really believe that this is causing failure.

The bride's mother seemed very happy and said, "Regardless of the fact that the groom is a dog, we have performed all the usual ceremonies for this. We respected the dog as we respected the human, and we spent the money as we did on real weddings. ".

According to tradition, Mingli has to take care of the dog for only a few months, after which he will be left alone.

The man who married a cow

On the Indonesian island of Bali, villagers once caught a young man named Njura Allit dressed for sex with a cow in a field. The young man told them that the cow seduced him, he said that she was beautiful and graceful, so he did not hold on and did what he did! ..

It was a more terrible excuse than sin. The villagers said to the boy: since you love the cow so much, you must officially marry her.

Indeed, they forced the young man to marry a cow in official ceremonies and in the presence of a large number of villagers.

Poor Nagura, during the wedding he passed out, and his mother screamed and turned on him ..

Some said that he passed out because of his shame over his scandal, which became "jalajel" until the press wrote about it, while others said that the joy of his relationship with his lover had lost his senses! ..

Unfortunately, this great love story between humans and cows was not always written for her. After a period where the bride's man slipped and fell into a deep barmaid and died drowning, and it is said that Njura was deeply saddened to lose her until he vowed that he would not marry her and remain faithful to her mention. life .. Who knows .. Perhaps if he had continued with her more, she would have become "the mother of his children."

A similar story happened in South Sudan in 2006 and attracted a lot of attention to his group, this time the bride was a goat, not a cow! ..

The British BBC published the news quoting a local newspaper in Juba. According to the newspaper, the owner of the goat Mr. Al-Yafi woke up late at night with reprehensible voices emanating from his barn, and he rushed there to find a naked man dressed in his goat, Rose. Mr. Alifi grabbed a man, his name was Toby, and then called the village elders to decide what to do about it.

The elders discussed the case for a while and then made this decision: Mr. Al-Yafi should not turn Toby over to the police. Instead, Toby is forced to marry a goat whose honor has been tarnished, and he has to pay Mr. Levy's dowry 50 dollars.

Toby actually married a goat and lived with great happiness for a while, but the hand of predestination refused to distinguish between them. The lovely goat died after a while while eating lunch in the village's trash bin .. She suffocated from a plastic bag! ...

Beware of the car rapist

What would you do if your car was raped? .. The question, which at first glance may seem stupid, but believe my dear reader that there are people who love cars so much that they do not hesitate to have sex with them when they have the opportunity!

One of these madmen named Edward Smith - 63 years old - from England, says that he first lost his virginity when he was a fourteen-year-old teenager who lost it with his white neighbor Volkswagen's car. Since then, he has not stopped having sex with cars, he has done so with more than seven hundred cars .. His passion was not limited to cars, but extended to motorcycles, buses, locomotives and even helicopters.

Of course, we're talking about real practice here, not just fantasy. A man treats cars like girls, hugs their tires, takes their lights and does other things that we cannot talk about.

Mr. Smith is currently married to a white Volkswagen vanilla, a relationship that has been going on for thirty years, he says he first saw him in 1982 and was in love at first sight.

Mr. Smith admits that he had transient relationships with real girls during periodic periods of his life, but she never lived to see a serious relationship, love of cars has always prevailed in his love of people.

In fact, mister. Smith's case is not unique, as he has a type of homosexuality called mechanophilia or machine love. This is a type of anomaly that is a crime in Britain and its owner is punished with imprisonment if caught raping the cars or cars of others.

You can say that mr. Smith is crazy .. But let me introduce you to someone who is crazier than him. Miss Amy Wolf (33) didn't like the car or the helicopter .. I even loved the magic carpet cart at the theme park! ..

Yes, dear reader .. Believe it or not .. Amy is in love with the cart and looks at it like a real man.

Amy met her lover - the cart - for the first time when she was 13 years old, and about this she says: "I immediately felt attracted to him sexually and mentally .. I love him as much as women love their husbands, and I know that we will be together forever. ".

Lolina has ridden her lover hundreds of times, she visits the theme park several times a month to be with her lover and she keeps a photo of him with her in her bed and she says that they and the cart have a strong emotional and physical relationship, but she is not jealous of others who ride her lover.

Amy is ridiculed from time to time, especially by her colleagues, but her family and friends support her, and about this she says: "I did not harm anyone with my love .. It's not my fault that I can't resist this, what should I do .. This is part of me. ".

Doll lover

Sex dolls are not something new, they were known in Japan and the West for a long time, they were previously made in the form of plastic dolls that blow with air, then they evolved with the development of technology and gradually became comparable to women in shape and texture .. Even speech .. Yes, some of them say, but of course they only say what the person wants to hear.

There are many stories of human love for dolls, perhaps the most famous of them is the story of the German old man Karl Tanzler, who was madly in love with a doll that he made himself, but in fact it was not an ordinary doll, rather the corpse of a girl who loved the old man to such degree that he exhumed her grave and took her body to his home and used dyes. The sticker turns her into a doll that divides his bed every night.

The story of old man Karl, which we touched on earlier in detail, but today we will talk with you about another man who was known for his passion for dolls until he became one of the most belligerent to spread and introduce people to the so-called synthetic Love.

Mr. Davikat met the love of his life in a nightclub, where he saw a woman who robbed his mind and heart, but she was not a real woman of flesh and blood, but a sex doll that the owner of the club offered to impress and surprise his clients. She was like a real woman, but she was made of plastic. Her painting did not leave Davikat's imagination, so he was determined to own someone like her, and worked hard for a year and a half until he collected her price, and it was not a small price, but he paid six thousand dollars, besides criticism for the American factory. specializing in making these "realistic" dolls.

They sent him a list of their products (in the form of a catalog), so he chose a doll named Sidori Koronko, and the next day the doll was with him.

Davikat's problem is that not only did he treat his doll like a sex doll, but his feelings developed for her over time, and he is emotionally attached to her as if she were his wife, it is true that they are not officially married because there is no court documenting human marriage to dolls, but he is very in love, and out of the seriousness of his love, he bought her boyfriend to entertain her unit while he is away from home. The new companion was, of course, only another sex doll named to us, and she also shared them with the bed .. why not .. As long as his wife does not mind! ...

Defecate says that he had previous relationships with human women and that it was these relationships that prompted him to be content with dolls. The doll does not quarrel, does not argue, does not require expenses, does not get sick, does not give birth, does not betray, etc. This sounds from the point of view of some men who want to have a companion for a mattress without responsibilities, who want the woman to make it the way they want.

As for the Devikat family, his mother reluctantly accepted his strange inclinations, while his father raged on just mentioning the doll's name.

The movie raised the issue of emotional relationships between people and dolls in the film Lars and the Realistic Girl, which won critical admiration and won some awards.

But if Devichat's love for his doll is somewhat understandable because of the human qualities of the doll, then South Korean love for Li Jin Chiu seems very far from understanding and logic, then a person loves his cheek! .. He officially married her in front of several guests and the media after wearing her wedding dress !! ..

Lee bought the pillow a few years ago, a large pillow imported from Japan featuring an anime girl named Testarossa.

"Lee" soon fell in love, his adoration of his cheek to mania and madness, take him for a walk, take her to the markets, sit next to him on the bus, and accompany him even while eating in a restaurant, ask her for food, as if she is a real person.

Such a strange love .. But wait .. There is something strange than this ..

A Japanese youth who called himself a journalist named Sal 9000 did not like a doll or a pillow. Rather, the love of a cartoon character exists only in an electronic game.

Sal met his girlfriend for the first time thanks to the famous Nintendo game on the device of electronic games, soon attached to the character and her lover, he takes her with him wherever he comes and goes, talking to him .. Save her .. He counts her your life partner.

The journalist asked him: "How can you love an electronic device?" .. Sal replied: "I love the character, not the device. I am fully aware that this is a game and I understand very well that I cannot marry her physically and legally. ". However, this did not stop Sal from applying for the marriage of his beloved metaphorically, thus becoming the first person in history to be associated with an electronic person, and several of his friends attended his wedding with some journalists. Of course, the bride was inside the gaming device, he asked to kiss her, kissing her picture in the car.

Mother loves her son's killer

The most serious thing that a mother can experience is the loss of one of her children, especially when his death is not fate and destiny, but rather an effective act, inevitably her heart will be filled with hatred and hatred for the person who deprived her of the pleasure from the liver. But that's incredible for Irish Audrey Fitzpatrick - 46 - who has decided to continue her marriage to a man accused of killing her son, stabbed to death.

The mother and killer were united by an eight-year relationship, which they were about to marry in 2008, but later this was due to the sudden and mysterious disappearance of Audrey's fifteen-year-old daughter, Amy, who had no trace. to this day. It happened in Spain when the family was spending time there, and the problem was widely known and still mysterious.

The mother struggled for years to find her daughter, to no avail, and then she was traumatized again last year after neighbors found the body of her 23-year-old son Dean, who was dumped outside her fiance, Dave Mohan, 43.

Religion was stabbed to death. The police charged Mohan and gathered enough evidence to bring him to justice.

But even though he faced trial for the murder of her son, and although his presence in her life was not synonymous except in disaster and disaster, Audrey is determined to marry Mohan no matter what, and she says of this: I love him, this is my stone on which I lean, and I am proud to be his wife. He knows that I love him to the bone, he knows that I am lost without him, I will die without him. ".

The irony is that the disappeared daughter was supposed to be her mother's bridesmaid during her wedding, while her murdered son was the one who brought her to the groom .. And now the runner-up is lost and the runner-up is under the mud ! .. But the wedding will go though.

Argentine Edith Casas - 22 years old - was no less determined than Urdu to continue her wedding, despite the outrage of people, Edith married not her son's killer, but the killer of her twin sister. In 2010, police found the body of her lovely sister Joanna Casas with two bullets to the head. The body was dropped on the outskirts of Beto Tonkado.

Two people were charged with the murder of a beautiful young woman who worked as a model and had a promising future. The first suspect is Victor Kangluni, her ex-boyfriend, and the second is Marco Diaz, who is her housing partner.

Victor was convicted of Joanna's murder and sentenced to 13 years in prison. But this did not lower the curtain on our story, as it exploded again when the dead sister announced that she was in love with her sister's killer and intended to marry him, despite all objections.

A court judge, at the request of the girl's mother, temporarily suspended the marriage procedures pending Edith's presentation to a psychiatrist to ensure her mental integrity.

The psychiatrist said Edith was sane and knew what she was going to do, that is, marry her twin sister's killer.

Despite all objections, the marriage took place in 2013, but Victor and Edith faced a lot of angry people at the gate of the courtyard that held their marriage, people poured rotten eggs and stones at them, forcing Victor to run disguised from the back door of the courtyard, he went straight into his cell to complete the remainder of his sentence.

Edith insists that her husband is not her sister's real killer, she says that he is innocent, although he was officially convicted by the court, but Edith's family has a different opinion, her father told reporters when he stopped crying: "Joanna went with God and Edith went with the devil. "As for her mother, said:" There are no phrases that could describe what Edith did, she is guilty of a terrible betrayal of her family and her sister's memory. "

The mother who married her son

Perhaps the most abhorrent sexual relationship between incest is that people are encouraged to talk about it as much as possible, and it is considered one of the most taboo in most cultures and religions. But in 2013, a Zimbabwean woman was struck by the world when she turned to her city council to agree to her marriage to her 23-year-old son Faray.

Mpriko's widow mother - 40 years old - said that her sexual relationship with her son began three years ago and that she is now six months pregnant with his child, that is, she will be the mother of a child who will give birth to him and find him at the same time !! ...

It was incredible not only because of his holiness and homosexuality, but also because of the woman's courage to apply for a formal marriage with her son ..

The mother responded to the protesters and deniers of her relationship with her son, saying, "Look ... I fought and tried my best to send my son to school and no one helped me. Now you see my son working and making money and accusing me of doing something wrong .. Let me enjoy the fruits of my efforts and ethnicity. ".

The strange thing is that the son no less wanted his mother to complete the marriage, he turned to the city council with the words: "I know that my father did not complete the payment of my mother's dowry to her family before his death, and I am ready to pay the remaining amount to my grandfather in exchange for consenting to my marriage to her, it is better to make it public. People should know that it was I who made my mother pregnant so that they would not accuse her of prostitution. ".

The amazing village council president told them that what they were saying was very ugly and that he would return with eternal damnation to the entire city. And that in the past, if something like this happened, they would be killed immediately. Today, people are afraid to break the law and do not want to intervene in problems, so they have two options that are not third for them: either immediately end their sinful relationship, or immediately leave the city. They decided to choose the second option, so they left the city and no one knows what happened to them after that.

Australia witnessed a similar story many years ago, but it was the opposite, the father wanted to marry his daughter. John Davis - 61 - Sexually involved with his daughter Jenny - 39 years old - with her consent and has two children.

Jenny says she hopes people will look at their relationship naturally and be respected and understood. But what the daughter asks for seems out of reach, as her relationship with her father has brought them to court.

The judge said that they can still see each other as father and daughter, but that it prevents them from engaging in any sexual activity because it would undermine the foundation of family and fatherhood.

Jenny's mother divorced her husband John when he was imprisoned for theft. Jenny hadn't seen her father for many years and she didn't date him again until 2000 when she was married and had two children.

Jenny says that there was physical attraction between her and her dad the first time they met, and that they had sex just two weeks after they met, Jenny described the relationship, saying, "My relationship with John is like another man's." ...

John, who was married at the time, said that he felt that what he was doing was wrong, but he finally gave in to his feelings.

Jenny left her husband, John left his wife, and they went to live together in southern Australia. But doubts arose about them after the birth of their first child, who suffered from a birth defect in his heart, which made him need a heart transfusion. They are subject to investigation and trial.

Forbidden issues of adultery always cause fuss when exposed because they are simply against human nature, even if love accompanies them, they remain unacceptable to most people. I am sure that most cultures and nations have banned and prevented incest, and sometimes even marriage between relatives such as cousins and aunts, because people have learned from hundreds of thousands of years of experience that marriage of relatives increases the likelihood that children will result from this marriage. have physical and mental illness and disabilities due to gene similarity

One of the most famous questions in this regard is the case of the German Patrick Stubink and his sister Susan.

Patrick was born in 1977 to a poor German family, took him out of the family at the age of three after his drunken father stabbed him with a knife, and the Stubinks adopted him at the age of seven and did not know anything about his real family - the Karolsky family - until 2000, when he first met his mother, and she died Mother a few months later from cancer.

After the death of his mother in 2001, Patrick's relationship with his sister Susan Karolsky, then sixteen years old and suffering from mental problems, deepened, gradually the relationship became sexual and began to live together, and Susan soon became pregnant with her first child.

The relationship between Patrick and his sister was discovered at the birth of their first child. The nurse complained that the child's father was the mother's brother. She called the police and Patrick was arrested and sentenced to ten months in prison for incest.

When Patrick was released from prison, he resumed his relationship with his sister and got Susan from him again, and again Patrick was arrested and sentenced to two and a half years in prison.

The relationship between the two brothers resulted in four children, three of whom were handicapped with physical and mental disabilities and were under the care of the state, and the fourth child was healthy and lived with his mother and father. To avoid having more disabled children, Patrick underwent sperm cutting in 2004 to become infertile.

The relationship of the two brothers caused a sensation in Europe, and the press wrote about it in detail, because Patrick filed a lawsuit with the Supreme Court of his country asking him to uphold his right to marry his sister, he said that preventing him from doing so was incompatible with human rights. The basis of the claim was based on the fact that German law criminalizing incest was old and dated from 1871 and that it no longer kept pace with the spirit of the times. Because of this case, the German Judicial Council criminalized incest in 2012, prompting Patrick to file a case with the European Supreme Court, which also dismissed his case and upheld the German court's decision.

Incest occurs in all countries of the world, but it occurs in secret and is rarely agreed on by both parties. Most cases take the form of persecution and rape by force by brothers and fathers. But sometimes it happens without deliberate .. Accidentally .. As happened with the Brazilian Adriana - 39 years old - who always joked about the similarity of her mother's name to the name of her husband's mother Leonardo - 37 years old -.

They both did not know who his real mother was, they never saw her, the name was only mentioned in their birth document, so both of them were abandoned by his mother as a child and raised by another family. There were no more jokes between them, Leonardo jokingly told Adriana: "It seems that my mother is the same as your mother! ". But they never complained that it might be true, especially since the mother's name of both of them is Maria, it is a widespread name in Brazil, it looks more like a marriage with two in our countries and their mother's name is "Fatima Mohamed" .. Perhaps this similarity requires a laugh, but this is not strange at all, because both names, Fatima and Muhammad, are widespread.

Adriana and Leonardo were born in the same city. Adriana left the city when she first got married, she lived in another city for fifteen years and gave birth to three children, but she divorced and returned to her city.

Returning to the city, she met a young man named Lonardo, and soon they fell in love, who lived together as a couple, although they never officially married, and Adriana gave birth to a child with Leonardo.

Throughout her life, Adriana's dream was to find her real mother who watches long and vainly, finally naming a popular radio program in Brazil, this program helped reunite relatives and friends who had not seen each other for years. Adriana mentioned her mother's name, gave information about herself such as her date of birth and the place where she lived and grew up, and asked for help finding her mother, who had never seen her during her life.

After a while at work, Adriana received a radio call and was told that there was a woman with whom she wanted to talk.

Adriana spoke to the woman and hundreds of thousands of people listened to her live .. It was an impressive conversation, this woman was her real mother. Can you imagine the situation, dear reader .. The mother is crying .. And the girl is crying .. They get to know each other for the first time .. And live ..

During a short meeting that lasted a few minutes, Adriana asked her mother a question and I asked her, "Do I have other brothers and sisters?" The mother told her that she gave birth to a child two years after her birth, she left him in the same place as Adriana, and that this child's name was Leonardo.

Here the conversation stops .. There was only constant crying ..
Adriana is crying .. Finally, she grabbed a little and said in a cas-
ual voice: "I can't believe you're telling me this .. Leonardo is my
husband! ".

At the end of the meeting, Adriana said to the presenter: "What
should I do now?" .. I'm afraid to go home to find Leonardo, and
he doesn't want me anymore .. I love him so much. ".

But Leonardo stuck with his wife, or rather his sister, in the en-
d. They met with their relatives and said that they decided to
stay together as a couple, even though they were brothers, and
that the opinions of others did not concern or concern them.

"Of course, it would be different if we knew before, but we did
not know ... We met and loved each other. ".. Adriana said she
added:" We thought it was funny, we both have the same name
as our mother, but it's a common name .. We thought it was just
a coincidence. We have many plans together and nothing can
tear us apart. ".

In fact, among all the stories in this article, this last story
amazed me .. The two brothers had never seen each other, each
of whom grew up in a different home ... How about heaven,
they met and got married .. Out of the thousands of men in her
city Adriana was only fined by someone who was actually her
brother, whom she did not know .. They love and give birth ..
Then they reach their mother, who rejected them four decades
ago, to tell them that they are brother and sister .. I swear I've
only heard this story in Indian films and I've always scoffed at
these films and said they were full of exaggerations and lies ..

But it looks like I was wrong .. Real life can sometimes be even stranger than Indian films ! ...

THE MOST FAMOUS VICTIMS OF ANIMAL ADORATION

Many people were killed for their loved ones .. Their friends .. Their families .. Or maybe for other people they may or may not know .. Young people died in defense of their homeland .. Dying for the sake of other people or for the sake of their homeland, we are all sure that this is a form of heroism .. But when a person dies for his love for an animal, it really is a miracle of the time !! .. Come on, dear reader .. We open doors for stories that have not been forgotten .. We better start our topic (Diana).

1- Diane Fossey

A girl from people threw them in the direction of the animal world, who did not find the sons of her skin, except for the lack of confidence and trust, who was killed and who killed her sons of her gender, and not the second sex, mankind lacked those who were attributed to them (Diana),.

A cold night of San Francisco evenings in January 1932 led to the marriage of an insurance agent (George E. Fossey) From a model (Catherine Fossey) About the birth of a child Diana, the heroine of our story, Diana did not want to live in a single family, because the conflict between her the parents led to their divorce in 1938, and in the same year her mother Katherine was involved with a businessman (Richard Price) And she received custody of her daughter Diana, and these events were enough to paint Diana's poor life.

Richard, her stepfather, was unfairly strict with her until she sat with her mother at the dinner table, was not available to her, and her poor father George could not communicate with his daughter, as her mother worked to break contact between the girl and her a real father, without compensating her for this, which made Diana lose interest in the Emotional that a child should have in the palm of his parents, so Diana went to the animal kingdom, and at first she was seen attached to her golden fish, and then she went to more intelligent beings. horses, and she excelled in horse riding at an early age.

The days went by like this until Diana's comeback intensified and she became young and she graduated from high school and began university admissions procedures. She wanted to study veterinary medicine, but her stepfather looked at her again and made her study money and business at an economics college, apparently fulfilled his order, but let's remember my dear reader that Diana was a horse rider, and it seems that she learned some things from the horse as his passion, and here is the hero of our story, teeming with the blood of young people and the passion of horses and throwing orders and instructions from her stepfather over the wall, but the girl did not despair and did not retreat, but worked to turn the dream into reality, and also worked in the store and in the factory as a worker, and began to study veterinary medicine.

Once again, life seems difficult to her and poor religions were unable to study them during their second year of weakness in science subjects, but she studied professional treatment and graduated from the university in 1954 and worked in several hospitals, and despite all this, she did not forgot her love for animals, and the language of her state told the animals that we will remain faithful until she smiles at Our sky.

In the years that followed, after hard work for Diana, D, the Walker Islands, and hope and disappointment, she was able to raise money and travel to Africa and travel to the brown continent. She began her journey from Kenya in 1963, Tanzania, Democratic Republic of the Congo, which these days were filled with violent wars and massacres, forcing Diana to travel to Rwanda altogether in 1967, and there began new chapters in Diana's life story. where she was fined by mountain gorillas there, became the center of her attention for the rest of her life, and she became known to her individually and interacted with her, imitating her voices, and she has been studying these gorillas for 18 years.

In 1983, her famous book, Gorilla, Drew in the Fog, and fishermen killed several of her favorite gorillas, and here fierce legal battles began between Diana and her supporters from the conservationists, against the fishermen who hated Diana so much, some of them went to prison, and spoiled the trade for millions of them dollars.

December 27, 1985, On that morning, conservationists and gorillas woke up from tragedy, Diana's bad body was found thrown into her booth, after a criminal cut the wall of a booth and insulted innocent religions and killed them with evil killers, like the criminal was said to be. was the son of a fisherman who made Diana by imprisoning him for attacking and killing gorillas, he hanged himself in a cell and his son came for revenge.

In 1988, a movie commemorated Diana with a film named after her book Gorillats in the Fog. The film covered details of her life, and later a United Nations foundation called the Diana Fossey Foundation was used to protect mountain gorillas.

2- King Alexander the First

From Diana, we turn to Greece, the country of the Greeks, during this period it was like drowning in the fires of the First World War, which burns more and more, and the country of the Greeks was not protected from this, despite the attempts of (Constantine I) King of Greece at that time, so neutrality is his way of ridding his country of disasters and fear of war, but it is easy for the tripartite reconciliation countries to be satisfied (France - Britain - Russia) So, this was also in cooperation with the Prime Minister (Viterius Venizius) A coup against Constantine I and his crown prince (George) And expel them and bring his second son (Alexander the First) King of Greece in 1917.

Let me, dear reader, summarize for you the features of Alexander I, who was a young man of great dreams and a little and somewhat reckless work, and the defect was in the hands of a prime minister without powers, only a nominal king, but he did not disobey the prime minister, and he supported him with all his moves (Including dragging Greece to WWI and he was very fond of animals and most of him was his favorite dog in the family (German Shepherd) German, and from the seriousness of his passion and love for his dog, he donated my life for him.

It happened in 1920 when he was hiking with his dog in the national park of Athens, and while walking, two sick monkeys fought with his dog, so Alexander only intervened in the battle, was bitten by a monkey, and he fell ill and remained treated for 23 days when I started, signs of improvement show that he died of sepsis from the bite on October 25, 1920.

As if he had learned a lesson from life that "you did not survive the battle against the sick monkeys, as you risk dragging your country and your people into a world war." !!

3- Steve Erwin

His looks .. He laughs .. And his interactions with animals and the public .. This is difficult for anyone who has ever seen it .. These are Australian gentlemen Steve Irwin .. Wildlife Pioneer and Protector.

(Steve Irwin) Born 1962 in Victoria, Australia.

And day after day, the malik grows and twists his love for animals, and he loved the gifts from his parents, presented by the Payson snake, I understood what it was, and for three years I could cope with even the largest crocodiles, I was a volunteer, we will paint on the possibility of crocodiles from scary places (And there is still not everything in his creative park, which he later named (Australian Zopark) „.

Un was a participant in the protection of the animals, so not ale of products containing species of livestock.

In 1992, on behalf of an American woman (Terry Giron), Kotori are indistinguishable from him in pogo instructions to protect animals, and the couple continued to protect animals together, and our friend racked up a type of cap called moe imya, and created his famous pragram (crocodile hunter) in 1996.

In 1998, he had a daughter who named him after his beloved crocodile (Bendy) and since he inherited from his parents a love for animals that he inherited for his sons Bendy and Robert, born in 2003, and Steve has participated in many films related to animals such as (cameo) and (Dr. Dolittle 2) and many others.

It was time for his daughter to become the host of programs for animals like her father, who would be filming scenes of one of the episodes of the planned program (Bindi Jungle Girl) 2006 on the great reef of Queensland, and from those scenes was his foreplay and banter with stingray or (Sea demon or lips) All of these designations refer to a cartilage cartilage with a sharp tail. Whenever you feel in danger, do not hesitate to use it.

And during the fun with this fish, it happened if he did not take into account how the fish hit Steve with its tail and killed him, so he died in those moments at the age of 44, leaving behind 8-year-old daughter Bendy and his 3-year-old son Roberta and his wife, but the family remained a brave family and she followed everything the late parent did, the show aired in 2007 and Bendy passed on the family's love of animals to her brother Robert.

The last moments before Steve was killed by this fish ..

4- Marius Els

From Australia to South Africa and the same deadly love, this time the victim - forty South Africans of European descent (Marius Els) Poor Marius, who took from the hippopotamus - the most dangerous animal on the brown continent - was his pet (Humphrey) According to Marius, named his little 5 month old hippo, our friend adopted him and put 160 hectares of land at the disposal of this animal. He built an artificial pond for him and did his best to make Humphrey happy and his main concern was for years and Humphrey began to grow, gain weight and show his aggression as time progressed.

Marius' friends and wife recently started warning him about his spoiled animal. He attacked the old man and his grandson and narrowly escaped him, after hiding from him for several hours until he left so that we could safely cross, and tried to attack and attack the people on the golf course, and day after day it increased, but Marius it was hard to believe it. Rather, he said that some people find it difficult to understand the relationship between him and Humphrey, and did not like the idea that Humphrey could harm anyone, and he began posting pictures of himself when he joked with Humphrey, courted him and rode on his back like common mare, indicate that what is said about Humphrey is wrong.

There are only a few days left until the hour of truth, and on the fateful Saturday of November 2011, during the fun of Marius with the hippopotamus Humphrey, and without warning, Humphrey killed Marius and pulled him under the water, forgetting that Marius preferred him, forgetting about the beautiful days between his father and his son, Marius also described their relationship, thus folding the page of the last five years of Marius' life, which he destroyed by raising and caring for the animal he adopted when he saved him from the flood when he was five months old and For five years, Humphrey repaid the debt with a great debt and killed those who improved it, and fiercely defended it to the end. After he dropped the words of his wife, friends and people, he showed a wall for Humphrey.

5- Timothy Treadwell (Bear Man)

Timothy Treadwell) Handsome young man born in 1957 was a fan of animals, and he also has a sad story, which is no less tragic than the rest of the stories, how this young man was addicted to drugs, and began his addiction, as he was refused to play with the sitcom, and he remained addicted until 1980, when doctors saved him from a heroin overdose that nearly killed him.

After several days of suffering, a friend convinced him to go with him to see one of the types of bears to relax, and Timothy forgot his worries and his mother agreed to this trip, and since this place was created and the bears saw the beginning of a new life when he quit addiction and started working as an environmental activist and he stayed to defend (Bears care about her and spent 13 years with her full training in Alaska and in those years she met his girlfriend (Amy Hogngard), Who was a physician assistant and was born in 1965, Timothy was rowdy and recorded several violations at multiple locations from 1994 to 2003.

Violations were to visit bears and take tours to see them without prior permission, and he stood against the operation of an electric fence around his camp to protect him from bears, and he was not satisfied with any method of protecting him from bears other than a can of pepper spray, which he used to repel one of the bears attacking him once.

Although he warned him not to deal with bears and his attention, one night in October 2003, the end of Timothy and his girlfriend Amy was at the hands of one of the bears he was protecting, it was a very scary night and investigators found only a very shocking audio recording in which Timothy screams Amy during a bear attack on them at night, Timothy was 46 years old and Amy was 38 years old, while the attacking bear was 28 years old, the bear was identified, and the remains of Timothy and Amy were found in his belly.

THE GIRL WHO AMAZED DOCTORS AND CONFUSED SCIENTISTS

Lina is indebted as long as she is known as the youngest mother in the history of medicine ..

Lina was born in a small and remote village in the mountains of Peru in 1933, her story began when they noticed severe swelling in her abdomen and her parents thought she had a tumor. However, doctors at a small rural clinic were unable to diagnose the child's condition, so her father went to the capital, and after several tests, the doctor told them that she was seven months pregnant !!.

Introduce my dear reader .. A five year old girl .. She is pregnant! .. How can this be so? ..

But we have to take a moment, because Lina was not really a normal child from birth. She went through her first menstrual cycle at the age of eight months, and there are other sources that say she got up at the age of two and a half. Her breasts began to stand out at the age of four, and at the age of five, her pelvis began to expand.

Mina's mother believed that her daughter was suffering from touching evil spirits and that this was why these strange things had happened; But Lina's mother did not know that her daughter had a very rare disease in early adulthood in children.

Returning to pregnant Lina, doctor. Gerardo Losada monitored her condition and took her to several places, including the capital, Lima, to confirm her pregnancy with obstetricians and gynecologists who supported that she was already pregnant.

A month and a half later, Lina gave birth to a male child 14-5-1939 who gave birth to him with a cesarean section for her small pelvic bones and her birth was supervised by a doctor. Losada, doctor. Posalio and anesthesiologist Dr. Colrita. The baby was born healthy and weighed 2.7 kg at the time, and the boy was named after Gerardo after the doctor who took care of Lina.

But who is the father of the child?

The police initially suspected Lina's father and arrested him for incest, but he was later released due to insufficient evidence and still no one knows who the child's father is, so when asked, Lina did not give an exact answer, which caused some come to the conclusion that she really did not know who the father of the child was, after all, she is only a five-year-old girl.

The child grew up that Lina was his sister, not his mother, but he discovered the truth when he was ten years old, and the doctor. Gerardo Lina and her son helped even after birth and supervised their education, and after many years Lina worked as a secretary as well as a doctor's assistant. Gerardo, who took care of her condition for a long time.

Later in her life, Lina married Raul Horado, who gave birth to her second son in 1972, and her first son was 33 years old. Unfortunately, the life of the first son did not last long. Gerardo died seven years later from bone marrow cancer in 1979.

Doubts and suspicions

For many years, people questioned Lina's pregnancy, many experts and scientists could not believe that a five-year-old girl could have full genitals and become pregnant, some said that all this was just a lie, or perhaps rumors, and that Gerardo was her brother really.

The New York Times published an article explaining the impossibility of carrying a five-year-old girl, but rather a doctor. Edmundo Esomel documented her condition in La Press Medica and explained that Lina is not an ordinary child and that her IQ is higher than that of children of her age, and also explained information about her rapid physical development.

Far from all these contradictions, there are documents that confirm the truth and validity of Mina's story. First, there are X-ray photographs of her uterus during pregnancy, as well as a photograph of her in her seventh month of pregnancy when she is naked. This picture clearly shows the development of her body and its differences from the bodies of other children of her age. She has full breasts and her belly is no doubt about her pregnancy. This is in addition to the many reports written by doctors who have carefully studied Lina's condition, as well as several photographs of Lina and her son.

There is very little early childhood maturity, but it does not exist.

Lina lives today with her husband in a dilapidated house in one of the poorest suburbs in the capital, Lima, this forgotten suburb is called "Little Chicago" because of the many crimes in it.

The government promised to provide us with financial assistance, these promises were repeated over the years, but Lina did not receive a dime and still lives in extreme poverty.

In fact, Lina got nothing from her strange story, other than perhaps horrible irony and rumors that affect her dignity as a woman, which is what ultimately led her to disembark and not tell anyone about her story, and her last contact with the press was in 2002, when she refused to speak to one of the TV channels that knocked on her door and never showed up after that.

One of the American newspapers said that if Lina's story happened in America, Lina would have a lot of fame and money, and doctors and scientists would rush to her, but in poor Peru, Lina received only pain and harm.

It is worth noting that Lina is not the only child in the world who gave birth at an early age. Ukrainian Liza Grishchenko was six years old when her 70-year-old grandfather raped her. A few days after celebrating her sixth birthday in 1934, she gave birth to a lovely baby weighing 3 kilograms. The birth was carried out naturally, rather than by caesarean section, as in the case of Mina, but, unfortunately, the newborn died a few minutes after her birth. He does not know what happened to Lisa after that, when she moved with her family to another place, possibly to avoid a scandal, and the family took the rapist's grandfather with them.

Another documented case is that of an Indian girl who was named by the press (H) Where her real name was hidden, the child took her to the hospital because she was suffering from excruciating stomach pain and she was six years old and her cases were diagnosed as a pregnancy amid the astonishment of her parents and doctors, and it is not known who caused her pregnancy, but she gave birth to a healthy baby girl in a hospital in Delhi in 1932, the birth was by caesarean section. Unlike Mina, the Indian girl was not a sign of puberty as her breasts were as small as any child of her age, but the odd thing is that she could breastfeed a baby from her breast after birth.

There are many other stories of girls who gave birth at the age of seven, eight and nine. But until today, the world did not know a child who gave birth to five years old, except for Mina.

Before we end this topic, a dear reader may ask, "Who is the youngest father in the world?"

The answer is that the world's youngest father is a nine-year-old man who married an 8-year-old girl in China in 1910 and had four children together. At that time, child marriage was very common in China and Southeast Asia. Unfortunately, I did not find this child's name or official document to support his story, nor did I find any children this age or younger who became parents. But there are documented stories of children who became parents after ten years. British child Saint Stewart became a father at the age of twelve, and the press called him the youngest father in the world, and had a sexual relationship with fifteen-year-old neighbor Emma, and then Emma married another man while Sen grew up and ended up in prison.

Another story known in Britain by a thirteen year old boy named Elf Patten, who had a child with his fifteen year old girl-friend, who claimed that Patten slept with her as the father of the child. At that time, the press wrote a lot about this story and promised her a miracle, especially since the features of the Elf were very childish. But the case brought many surprises as the Elf's mother did not believe that her son was the father of the child, so she insisted on DNA testing, which showed that Elf was not the child's father and that the father of the real child was a teenager at the age of fifteen. years.

I personally think there are many stories of mothers and fathers of children, perhaps even at a younger age than we mentioned in this article, but many of these stories have not been documented, perhaps to avoid a scandal, gossip.

WHO SAID MEN ARE UNFAITHFUL?

The accusation we have always heard of women hesitating with some splendor that men are not fulfilled and they lasted, worked out, and were guilty of repeating this accusation, and one of them said (like an Egyptian) what he believes in people are like those who provide water to strangers, and of course water never stands in a sieve. Another (possibly as a Moroccan) said that if a man dies, he looks for a new wife among the goats! .. Once I read a phrase that made me laugh, saying: if I see a man opening the car door for his wife, I know that one of them is new, or a car, or a wife !!. A metaphor of a person's interest only in the new and his inability to fulfill the old. On the other hand, men say they are more loyal than women, and there is evidence that the wife often misses her husband in front of others, especially her friends, while the husband rarely speaks badly about his wife in front of his friends. And that if a person truly loves, it is impossible to forget this love and will remain faithful to him throughout his life. But the problem here, according to one of the women, is that no one knows but God when a man truly loves, because he says to every new woman he meets: "You are the only love in my life."! ...

In my humble opinion, loyalty has more to do with a person's character and makeup than with their gender. There are faithful men, there are women who are dead, and vice versa. But overall, loyalty is a rare currency in our most difficult times, as it is not easy to deny promises and the quickest forgetting of covenants, and what is more ungrateful at a time when everything has gone digital. In the past, we walked miles and waited hours to see a friend, relative, or lover, but today we hardly call our mobile ... Maybe once a year.

Lack of loyalty these days makes a person stand firm and empty when he sees a position that indicates loyalty, dedication and pure love, free of interests and goals. Our story today is one of the wonderful stories of loyalty that leave their mark on feelings and conscience.

One sunny and beautiful day in 1937, a handsome young man named Rocky walked into a small street cafe in the Argentine city of Buenos Aires for a cup of coffee, sat at a small table and quietly sipped a cup while his fingers caressed the inscriptions of a white mattress lying on table in front of him. Meanwhile, two girls were sitting at the table, and the words of one of them greatly attracted his attention, her voice was sweet and her conversation was sweet and sweet, she was talking with her friend about deep things .. About how a person transcends his spirit, what is the meaning of his life and how he faces all his problems and problems with a good word and useful work .. Her conversation was exciting.

"Before I even turn back to see her face, I told myself that this girl is mine and I have to get to know her," says Rocky. He immediately realized as soon as he turned to look that he had found his soul mate, besides the sweetness of her voice and the sweetness of her speech and soul, her beauty was beautiful and exciting.

"It was pure love." .. Rocky recalls this moment and understands: "Her beauty was an additional gift, a reward."

Her name is Juliet, an Argentine beauty, Rocky won her heart and he won the grand prize.

They were associated with fiery love, which ended in marriage and had two children, a beautiful boy and a girl.

And unlike most love stories that we hear or live about ourselves, the love of Rocky and Juliet did not die after the wedding and was not weakened and weakened, on the contrary, the more time passed, the closer it gets and becomes stronger and more consistent.

In 1971, Rocky and his little family immigrated to the United States and settled in Boston. There, his son found a job in another state, married his daughter and left the house, so the couple was left alone, but this unity did not interfere with them and did not make them happy, but they were very happy, with every sunrise, all their love is born over.

Unfortunately, nothing lasts .. In 1993, after 55 years of marriage, this great love story reached its final stop. Juliet suffered from heart disease and died of complications and was buried in Saint Joseph's Cemetery, a cemetery near the couple's home.

With Juliet's death, Rocky drowned in deep sadness, tears did not leave his eyes, he restored food and drink ... what will he do now? How would he spend his life without his soul mate? ...

"It is impossible to leave Juliet, it is impossible to live without her." .. So Rocky told himself, and so he decided to stay with her grave until it was his turn to sleep next to her forever.

Every morning, as soon as the St. Joseph opens his doors, Rocky enters first, walking quickly between the graves until he reaches Juliet's grave, greeting her, saying, "Hi, dear ... I'm here." Then he sits next to the grave and stays with him until evening the cemetery closes its doors.

The atmosphere doesn't matter .. Free .. cold .. Rain .. snow .. Storms .. Doesn't matter .. Nothing stopped this stubborn, slender Argentinean old man from his beloved grave who didn't leave her, no matter what happened, on holidays, he brings her gifts, lights candles, and distributes cake to cemetery visitors on their wedding anniversary. He was afraid that she would feel lonely and tired, trying to save her and entertain her, and sometimes he would sing for her. In the evening, when the date of his departure came, some news and grains were scattered over the grave, so the squirrels came and ate them .. And about this he says: "I do not want her to feel lonely and lonely after my departure .. Therefore I put squirrel food to come and have some fun. ".

Years pass, and this old man, sitting on the grave of his wife, does not budge, despite being ninety years old. Visitors to the cemetery and residents of neighboring houses began to notice his constant presence: what is his story? .. Why is he all the time, is he crazy? .. Everyone asked. Yes, he's crazy .. His wife loved him and separated his girlfriend ..

"It's part of me, so when I'm here I feel complete." .. "My presence here makes me feel better, it doesn't compensate for her loss, but I feel better here."

Many visitors to the cemetery began to approach the old man and ask him curiously about his story, and Rocky was not upset with their questions, on the contrary, he was a good person who welcomed everyone, he told his story, and told them anecdotes and attitudes of his memories with Juliet .. Some of them suffered a lot, cried while others disappeared, and they were incredible in the kind of love and devotion that the old man had for his late wife.

Gradually people came to bring flowers to put on Juliet's grave and they took pictures with Rocky, and soon the press came and history became every language.

In 2013, Rocky's story reached its sad conclusion .. And happy in the same now, Twenty years after his wife's grave was attached, Rocky never came to the cemetery as usual, He fell ill and fell into bed, But he did not look back ago, A month later, he came back again, This time he no longer sits next to Juliet .. No .. But sleeping next to her .. Yes, the old lover finally died .. They buried him next to his wife, to her left as he asked them in his will, just as they stood before the altar on their wedding night in 1937 ..

Now Rocky won't have to leave his girlfriend when the evening comes and the cemetery closes its doors .. Because they will be there forever.

SEXUAL TRANSFORMATION: KNOWN ISSUES AND ONGOING CONTROVERSY

Sexual transformation (Transgender) This is very briefly the transformation of a person from one sex to another.It, from masculinity to femininity and vice versa, The motive is often a disease known as sexual identity disorder, caused by problems in the functions of the brain and reproductive system, imbalance in the work of the glands and secretion of the hormone, so that the injured feel that it belongs in terms of feelings, feelings and tendencies, And sometimes the participants, For a different gender. Of course, this condition is mostly at birth, it shows its signs and symptoms in childhood and becomes more ingrained over time, leading to great suffering, so that the injured often tend to band together and move out of peers of the same gender and show symptoms of depression and anxiety. ...

Ethically, legally and legally, there is a lot of disagreement about sexual transformation between the strong supporter, the conservative and the outright rejected. Each team has its own arguments and evidence. On the social side, most people experience an unacceptable feeling and shock when they associate with a transsexual, so these converts often keep their business secret and can only know about their past, close to them and their families.

Sexual transformation is not easy, I mean not only physically, but also psychologically, because it does not adapt to the new life and the difficulties of integration and the worldview of society, in addition to the financial costs and side effects of surgeries and hormone therapy .. All this can lead to breakdown of a transsexual and can lead to cases of depression, mental illness, nervous breakdowns and suicide, and there are even transsexuals who later regretted their transformation and returned to their previous sex.

All in all, in our article, we will take a quick look at the most famous problems of sexual transformation around the world, noting that some of those we touched on did not become fully sexual, but they lived and acted for a long period of their lives as a different gender where they were born, Others have been transformed for reasons other than sexual identity disorder.

Matthew Crozlesky .. Iron Woman

Scary human monster, muscle mass, world weightlifting record, guard of former US President Bill Clinton, famous champion of physical strength competitions, married twice and has three children .. These are some of Matthew's qualities and achievements .. Super man, as he was called, no longer a man! Rather, he turned into a woman named Jenny Kroc, and his transformation shook the world of bodybuilding and weightlifting. Matthew lived for several years, hesitating between two characters, one of which is superman, and in the other he is a thin woman, and he described this internal conflict, saying that he felt the presence of two completely different people, fighting and fighting for control of their bodies. It seems that the female character has finally won .. Thus, the world champion, lifting weights, turned into a woman named Jenny.

Bruce Jenner .. From National Hero to Magazine Cover Woman

He is arguably one of the most prominent transsexuals due to his glorious past, and since he also belongs to a famous family, he is the husband of the mother of famous reality TV star Kim Kardashian. His transformation has sparked a lot of controversy and issues with magazine covers and television program titles.

Bruce, in his sixties, was a sports hero in his youth called Lebanon, the American people applauded him enthusiastically, and the presidents warmly welcomed him to the White House as he is the world champion in athletics, broke many records and won many gold medals. Bruce married his life as a man of 3 women and has 6 children. But he surprised the world with his recent transformation as a woman and called himself Caitlin Jenner.

Transforming fashion models

Perhaps the dear reader will be surprised and amazed when you learn that some of the most prominent models and beauty queens were once men! ..

Carmen Carrera is one of the most famous models, but she was originally a man, and Carmen says: "I always took pictures of myself and over time I realized that my face is very beautiful, so I decided to switch to a girl." .. Later it becomes one of the most outstanding models

Leah T is one of the most famous Brazilian models, originally a young man named Leonardo, but decided to turn into a girl and take part in the fashion world.

Claudia Chariz is one of the most famous models of the American fashion agency Janice Dickinson, but she is originally a mutant.

There are many others and the list goes on .. But unlike these men who turned into women, Ashton Colby, Blonde American Belle, who competed in several Miss competitions, She was a candidate for the title of Miss America, She decided to leave fame. Money, and looks admiration behind her back and turns into a man, She underwent surgery to completely remove her breasts, She released a beard after several months of taking male drugs and hormones, She says that she is now happier and never skips makeup and dresses.

The first person in the world to conceive of Wild

Thomas Betty was hustling around in 2002. Every newspaper in the world reported the news about this "pregnant" man, and his bloated belly image made all the headlines .. At first it was a shock for men, But the picture soon became clear after Thomas's past was revealed, He was not born a human. Rather, he saw the light of day as a woman named Tracy, Not an ordinary woman, But miss, Tracy won a teenage beauty pageant in Hawaii, But later she decided to turn into a man and then married a woman named Nancy. And because Nancy was infertile, and because Tracy, or rather Thomas, still retained her female genital system, it was therefore decided that Thomas would be pregnant instead of Nancy.

But if the husband is a woman and the wife is a woman, then who is the father of the child? ..

Unidentified father, the man who donated his sperm to the couple. For your information, Thomas gave birth to not one child, but three, and the news was released again after he divorced his first wife and married another, Empere.

Conchita Rest .. bearded lady

She gained attention during the 2015 European Eurovision Singing Contest when she won first place. She was born in 1988 as a man named Thomas Neuworth and the press dubbed her "The Bearded Lady" because after the transformation of the woman she kept a beard and she does it as an expression of tolerance and acceptance of the other. Conchita says that as a teenager she suffered a lot of persecution and racism and then decided to switch to a woman.

Chevalier Divoir Ion

I don't know if you've watched Lady Oscar.It's a popular animated series that tells the story of a French girl who lived most of her life as a man.The story is based on the life of a French spy who lived in the eighteenth century and occupied people all his life. only because of his achievements, But because of their confusion about being a man or a woman, How he lived most of his life as a man, Participated in wars, He was very skillful in swordsmanship, He became one of the king's knights, He then lived another remainder of his life as a woman.He worked as a bridesmaid for the Empress of Russia and followed her for the French government, Then he returned and worked as an ambassador and spy in England as a man.In conclusion, he returned to France to live the remainder life as a woman, claiming that he was a female child and that his father raised him as a child so that the family would not lose their property due to the lack of a male heir. what gender. The puzzle Chevalier confused people all their lives, Even after his death, people were confused, The doctors who examined his body were stunned, On the one hand, he had a fully developed male reproductive system, Which means that he is a man. On the other hand, he possessed female deities, the most important of which was the presence of a fully developed breast.

Arab converts

Of course, sexual transformation has nothing to do with nationalism, culture, religion, etc. Rather, it has to do with the mental and physical makeup of a person. Sexual transformation is one of the things that is tolerated in our Arab world.The conservative nature of society prevents most transgender people from professing their transformation, But from time to time there are bold problems and situations that have succeeded in explicit presentation, through social media or through television programs and meetings. These cases are often met with condemnation and disapproval of society's rejection of the idea of sexual transformation.

Perhaps the most famous Arab transsexual is the late artist Hanan Al-Tawil, who was known to the public for her light blood in several cinematic roles, the most famous of which was the role of a Korean dancer in Askar in Camp, starring artist Muhammad Hennedy. Hanan gave birth to a man named "Tariq" and she lived for a long time as a man, but with feminine inclinations and behavior, before deciding to go to a woman forever through operations, then she went into the world of show and acting and she achieved success and won the admiration of the people. But as it suddenly appeared, she also suddenly missed in 2004 to shock people with the news of her death, which was shrouded in mystery.There are those who said that she died of a heart attack, There are those who said that she died of suicide.Perhaps the second statement is more likely because it was still relatively minor for heart disease as she died only 38 years old. Note that many trans people develop severe depression and may commit suicide due to their community outlook or love relationship that ends in failure when the other party knows the reality of the trans.

Dancer Nour is another famous and brave case in our Arab world, Where I was born a man named "Nurdin". She says that from an early age she felt different from her peers and inclination to play and communicate with women. She soon discovered that she is hermaphrodite, This, he has a male and female genitals at the same time, In conclusion, after much suffering, it was decided to carry out a correction of her sex in Switzerland in 2004, from Nureddin to Nur, From man to dancer, Even the ambassador of Oriental dance! Soon, her star was shining and appearing on many television programs to speak frankly about her condition, which is the envy of many transgender people in our Arab society.

Bornisha women

This is a group of women in rural Albania and parts of the Balkans who live the life of a man all their lives, wear clothes that belong to men, and cut their feelings just like them. They also carry all the responsibilities and tasks that men perform. They are also called: "Department of the Virgin.", Because they swear by their youth - with the consent of their families - that they remain virgins throughout their lives and never have sex, This section is in front of 12 people from the village or city elders, Then a girl can live like men and enjoy all her privileges and freedoms, Porinshe women are allowed to smoke, drink alcohol, carry a gun, and communicate with men .. But .. If a Virgo breaks her oath and has sex, her punishment is death.

Currently, the number of births is very small and they are all elderly, this habit originated from the past and the death penalty is no longer applied to the wicked virgin in her department. This Porinshi tradition originated many centuries ago, As those who follow this tradition are women who lost their dependents from their married men, they had to do the job, As for some women, they follow this tradition in order to gain more freedom, They live in conservative rural areas that prevent women from doing things. In conclusion, there are families that force their daughters to become burnish for the sake of inheritance, since rural societies do not allow women to receive their inheritance, especially in relation to land, Therefore, so that the family does not lose their land in the absence of a male heir, one of the daughters of the family is represented by Bornichet Because Purnisha women have the right to own property just like men.

The bottom line is that Purnisha women are not transgender women, they have not made a transformation, but they have lived most of their lives as men in terms of form, behavior and privilege.

THE FATHER WHO SHOOK THE WHOLE WORLD!

Joseph Fritzel was born on April 9, 1935 in the city of Amstetin, an Austrian from a poor family where his mother worked as a domestic servant and his father abandoned them when Joseph was four years old. Joseph was the only son of his mother, who was very cruel to him, beat him and constantly insulted him, and Joseph said that he was always humiliated because of this treatment from his mother .. Under all these harsh conditions, he completed his education and earned an electrical engineering qualification from college, and when he turned 21, he took a job with an electronics company and married a 17 year old girl named Rosemary, and they had 7 children .. 5 girls and two boys.

Joseph had a different aspect of his life besides the one that everyone knew as a respectable head of the family and a working man. He had a history of rape, the first of which was in 1967, when he stormed the house of a young nurse in the absence of her husband and raped her under threatened with a knife, and he was later convicted of rape and sentenced to 18 months in prison.

In 1977, Joseph began stalking his eldest daughter, Elizabeth, then 11 years old. When Elizabeth was 15, she decided to run away with her boyfriend to get rid of her father's hell, and she did manage to escape, but a few weeks later the police returned her to her father because she was underage .. What a paradox .. The police returned the victim themselves and gave it to the monster! ..

Elizabeth's real torment began in 1984, when her father lured her into the basement of his house on the pretext to help him install and install an iron door, if Elizabeth did not realize at the time that the huge door that helped her father to install was actually her door. the cell in which she will live for 24 years. As soon as he finished repairing the door, he surprised his daughter and wetted a piece of tissue with anesthesia on her mouth, and she passed out.

Joseph had previously planned everything, and his job brought in a good income, which allowed him to buy a spacious house with two apartments, one of which was used to accommodate his family, and the other was rented. There was a cellar in the building, and Joseph secretly expanded that cellar, and he planned it during his time in prison for rape .. He wanted to set up a secret cell in the basement of his house to keep his next victim, so he first dug a long corridor branching from the basement, and made the door leading to this corridor completely disguised so that no one could distinguish it, since it was an electronic door in which there is not even a keyhole, but the remote control road has a password. Behind this disguised door are four other doors, each with locks, and behind these doors Joseph built his apartment or secret chamber, which contained a living room and two bedrooms with a bathroom and a small kitchen.

It goes without saying that the first victim of the launch of this secret chamber was only Joseph's eldest daughter, Elizabeth. After her parents lured her to the basement and drugged her, he kept her there, chained and raped her and she screamed a lot for help, but how her voice went out into the street when she was imprisoned behind five doors, even behind eight doors! There are three additional doors that separate the basement from the stairs leading up.

Elizabeth disappeared and no one saw her after her and her mother was very worried about her and she informed the police .. She did not know that her daughter was closer to her than she thought, sitting under her house, and when the police came investigate, Joseph told them that he had received a letter from his daughter stating that she had fled and joined the religious community and would never return, and Joseph forced Elizabeth to write this letter in his own handwriting before handing it over to the police.

Joseph continued to rape his daughter for many years and gave birth to seven children, one of whom died shortly after his birth, and Joseph burned his body so that it would not be found. It is estimated that Joseph raped Elizabeth over 3,000 times in 24 years, and sometimes these attacks took place in front of children, as Elizabeth said that her father sometimes forced her to watch pornographic films and then forced her to apply some of the scenes from those films to him before her children to humiliate her. He will punish her and her children if they make noise or refuse to follow orders to turn off the electricity and food for several days .. He did not visit them every day, but sometimes he did not go to the basement for several days, but on average he did come to them every three days to provide them with food and drink and to rape Elizabeth.

The strange thing about this case is that Joseph took three children whom Elizabeth had to live with him and his wife Rosemary and officially adopted them, and he deceived his wife, authorities and competent authorities found the children on the doorstep and decided to adopt them. ..

We can ask ourselves how during these years Rosemary did not feel the crime that took place in the basement of her house ?! ..

In fact, Joseph was delusional that he would go to the basement and spend time there developing electrical fees to sell to companies, and he emphasized that they did not go to him and boycotted his knowledge. Of course, it is impossible that she has never been in the basement for 24 years, inevitably she did this time, but as we mentioned, Joseph presented the door of the corridor leading to the cell to Elizabeth and her children so that no one could see and distinguish it. As for the neighbors, or rather the tenants that Joseph rented out on the first floor, they said they heard some suspicious sounds coming from the basement, but Joseph told them it was fired by the heater .. Joseph was a genius at deception!

The tragedy ends

Bitter and difficult years passed over Elizabeth in this damp and cold cellar, and her children grew older until they reached the age of youth, and knew from the world only that gloomy cellar in which they were born, they did not see the sky blue in their lives, and Elizabeth pleaded with her father to let them expand the cellar more because she and her children could no longer help, so he agreed and made her work with her children with her bare hands for years to dig the dirt and expand the secret cellar to 55 square meters.

The humidity and coldness in the basement caused many illnesses in the children, and the basement ceiling was low, causing Stephen, son of Elizabeth, to bend all the time after he reached the age of youth and exceeded his length of 173 centimeters, and this affected his spine, and Joseph himself was in charge of treating the children when they got sick and brought them medicine, but on April 19, 2008, the eldest daughter "Christina" fell ill and he was nineteen years old as she was suffering from severe kidney failure, then Elizabeth asked her father to take the girl to the hospital. and Joseph agreed to deliver an ambulance to the hospital, and forced Elizabeth to write a message to doctors explaining her daughter's health, and here the medical team questioned this, especially since they noticed that Christina seemed unnatural as her skin was pale and suffered from malnutrition, and she has no identification papers .. The police were informed and investigations began, while Elizabeth insisted ala and begged her father to take her to the hospital to check on her daughter, and Joseph agreed, but warned her not to open her mouth. On arrival, the doctor informed the police, and she rushed to the scene and began to question them ..

When the police began to investigate Elizabeth's cases, she indicated that she and her children would be insured and that she would never see Joseph again in exchange for confessing everything .. Investigators were informed of the whole story, Joseph was arrested and charged with illegal detention, rape and murder for negligence.

In the early morning of April 27, 2008, the police raided Joseph's house, the children were taken out and placed in preventive care, and the children saw the outside world and breathed fresh air for the first time in their lives.

Joseph confessed to psychiatrists that his thoughts of imprisoning someone began to crystallize while he was in prison serving a sentence for rape. Joseph's medical diagnosis of his condition was that he had a severe personality disorder in addition to sexual dysfunction and delinquency.

Elizabeth's brother, Harald Fritzel, testified that he was also the victim of the abuse of his father Joseph, who suffered a series of severe beatings as a child, while Rosemary's wife and the rest of his sons and daughters refused to testify.

During the trial, Joseph tried to show this as if he agreed with his daughter, saying that he is not a monster and that he cares for her and her children and brings them gifts, and that he kept her mostly for discipline, not for rape. Of course, these words did not convince anyone, especially after Elizabeth's lawyer presented to the jury some materials taken from the cellar cell, which I presented to the jury and asked them to smell, the smell of these materials was so unpleasant that the jury almost emptied their stomachs from the severity of disgust it was mold and the moisture in this lonely cellar is incredible. Is it reasonable that someone agrees to live in this rotten cell with his consent? ...

It was decided that Elizabeth would not be present at the trial in order to protect her from the press, and instead of attending in person, the police showed a video of her eight-hour testimony, and the details she revealed in this tape were so ugly and bad for my conscience. that the jury took turns hearing these details every two hours.

Most of those present at the trial did not know that Elizabeth was present at one of the sessions, and she was present when part of her testimony, taped, was broadcast, in fact, she was sitting disguised among the audience who were present at the trial, but her father, sitting in the indictment, recognized her and felt her presence, and he showed confusion.Paleness immediately, and soon he announced that he had confessed to all charges against him except the murder charge, and stated that he would agree with the court's decision and will never apply for amnesty. Indeed, he was sentenced to life imprisonment with parole after 15 years and is now serving a sentence in the mentally ill prison section in an Austrian prison.

As for Elizabeth, she and her children went through a long period of psychological and physical rehabilitation, not only with her and her children who lived with her in the basement, but even the three children that Joseph took and adopted with his wife Rosemary, they were also seriously injured after learning that their mother who raised them was in fact their grandmother and that their father was their grandfather who raped their real mother, imprisoned in the basement under the house where they were brought up.

The relationship between Elizabeth and her mother was tense, Elizabeth became very angry with her mother and interrupted her because she believed her father's words that she left home and joined a religious community and did not try to look for her for 24 years, but she made peace with her later and allowed her to meet her three sons, who raised her themselves.

Currently, according to the latest news, Elizabeth lives quietly with her children in a city in northern Austria, and they have been given new identities so that no one will recognize them, and their house is guarded around the clock to ward off intruders.

The case of Joseph Ferzl caused a great shock throughout the world, and this is perhaps the most important issue that contributed to the coverage of the problem of incest, and for science it is a problem that occurs in many societies, but is silent about it, it is one of the most taboo, and makes to think about how a person allows himself to commit sexual assault on a member of his house, this is indeed a diabolical desire and energetic whim in every sense of the word, and perhaps most of those who have committed these actions are people who are psychologically and emotionally disturbed. As for Fritzel, he told investigators that the cruelty he faced with his mother as a child had a devastating effect on his psyche, who fought, cursed and insulted him constantly, because for no reason, she was a very cruel woman and without feelings, he said that he never mentioned that she hugged him or accepted him at least once throughout his childhood, and one of the paradoxes of the time is that the verse was changed after Joseph became a young man how he became the one who brutalized his mother and beat her and kept her in the attic of the house and covered her windows with bricks and she stayed there twenty years before she died and no one saw or knew With her presence. ...

GENERAL AND
A BATTALION
OF WHORES

History is written by the winners, A proposal that diminishes many facts, From them, most of what we read about eternal battles, glorious championships, and the consequences of victories are just flower talks about building, And that the truth is often completely different, Each victory is compensated by loss. often paid for by the safe civilians in their villages and towns, which are ravaged by equestrian defenders and spreading destruction and terror everywhere. We hear and read about the courage and heroism of soldiers in battles, But they never tell us how many girls were killed or raped by these articulated heroes, This is the quiet aspect, Or rather acceptable, As long as we are the victorious party, As long as these women are not our mothers, sisters , wife and daughter.

The Nazis raped millions of women in the countries they conquered and occupied. These are crimes that have been documented and taught to people for generations. To be honest, this is not a lie or an invention, but, on the other hand, the allies were not the angels of the two houses, but we hear little about the crimes of the allies .. Why? .. We go back and say: "History is written by the winners." ..

When the Third Reich fell in 1945, two million German women were raped by Soviet soldiers. It was a brutal rape with every cruel word you could imagine. And let's use the footage of a Russian officer here to film a small and quick scene of these atrocities, Where he tells us about entering Berlin for the first time, And as he roamed his bike around the edge when he saw a group of women carrying household items, He asked them why they left their homes, They looked at him with difficulties, one of them came forward, was a beautiful girl and said: "They raped me .. More than twenty people. "She pointed to the crying of her skirt, she said that some of her rapists were elders, her mother confirmed her words when she said:" They raped my daughter in front of me and they can come back to rape her again. "Then the girl she said begging: "Stay with me", rushed at me and said: "You can sleep with me, You can do whatever you want with me, But only you!" .. Poor girl, I begged that I was raped by one person in exchange for protection, which, of course, is better than rape by the dozens.

Of course, what these Soviet soldiers were doing was not a unique thing or an emergency in history. The Germans themselves brutally raped millions of Russian women when they invaded the Soviet Union in 1941. The brutality of the war and the inability to see women for months on the frontlines turned most men into broken human monsters, a fact known to military field commanders, and for this reason, some armies poured camphor oil into the drinking water provided to soldiers to reduce their sexual excitement. While other armies provide prostitutes to their soldiers to safely empty their sexual desires, perhaps the so-called "comfort homes" that the Japanese created for their soldiers during the invasion of Korea, China and other Southeast Asian countries are best known. in this area, Although the women who worked in these houses were not prostitutes, They did not receive a price for their services, To be forced, Housewives, workers and farmers are forcibly placed in these houses so that the soldiers can have sex with them whenever they want.

However, an American general named Joseph Hooker is not considering a new idea of providing sexual comfort to his soldiers, a peaceful idea by forming a battalion of prostitutes to serve as moral support! .. On the one hand, the soldiers are happy and feel comfortable and do not rape anyone, and on the other hand, the prostitutes are happy with the abundance of clients and the generosity of the price .. What a smart idea!.

It is said that this general's operating room during the American Civil War was the strangest in history, The operating room or command room is, as usual, full of military maps and officers immersed in discussions of the conduct of battles and plans, General Hooker's operating room was full of bottles of whiskey. gambling tables and prostitutes .. The weird thing is that General Hooker fought some of his battles while he was drunk .. It wins!.

History remembered General Hooker in a strange way, as the word "Hooker" entered the English dictionary in the sense of a prostitute and became an insult, especially in America.

Of course, there are historians who disagree with these words, and they consider this an exaggeration and distortion of the reputation of General Hooker, but despite this, the name of General Hooker will remain immortal in history as a synonym for prostitution and prostitution. Although I personally see that this man was somewhat smart and merciful to the many bastard soldiers who have raped women over the centuries.

Imagine that every army was accompanied by a "prostitute battalion" .. I don't think that a woman will be raped after her, and no one will run away from military service! ...

WONDERFUL DREAM .. STRANGE STORY THAN FICTION

In France and before the outbreak of World War I in 1914, Know It All (Sarah) And also (John) On each other, they fell in love, and the love between them was almost completed by marriage, if not for the First World War at the time, since John was an adult, he was drafted into the army and sent to the front and to the front line.

The two lovers stayed for two years despite the war and death, and the messages between them did not stop and continued for pages and pages.

Until the day when John's messages ceased completely and permanently, tragedy followed in a telegram informing Sarah and John's family that his battalion had been almost completely destroyed in one area in southern France and that her fiancé's name was among the missing , and most likely he died despite the fact that they did not receive his body, but the authorities told them not to hope for his survival

Sarah collapsed completely and cried all day until she was tired and slept with tears in her eyes, saddened by her fiance and the lost love of her life.

And that night I had a dream that changed the course of her life forever.

Sarah dreamed that she was walking in the countryside, and there was a building on the horizon, and when she approached the building, she fainted when it was once a majestic castle, and for the seriousness of her joy she found John standing next to with this castle, She rushed to him, ran to hug him and hug him, but before she reached him, she saw a shell hitting one of the castle's towers, and for her horror, she found that debris fell on the head of her fiance, so she rushed to the place of the wreckage to hear the voice of John who calls her to save me ...

Sarah jumped out of the dream in horror, the dream was incredibly real, as if she could still smell the flying mud and almost hear the sound of her lost love, but she is a normal girl and knows that this dream is nothing more than a dream.

She came back and laid her head on the pillow to sleep so she could dream again with the same details!

"No, that's impossible. Sarah thought, but who among us has heard of the dream repeated twice? And with the same detail and intensity? If it doesn't matter or a message from heaven.

Then Sarah decided to go and find this castle, where she linked her opening of the castle with the search for her missing lover and informed her husband and family of her decision, but they all opposed it, since it is maddening to go to a distant country to look for a dead person because of sleep, but she did not listen to this discussion and thus strengthened the traveler to the last place. John Battalion was spotted in the countryside in southern France.

At that time there was little transport and the road was difficult and Sarah spent all the time on the road on foot, or if she found a car driven by a farmer who was traveling with him and told him a story to shake her head sympathetically, and Sarah went down to the nearest point ...

Two months later, Sarah arrived at her destination and started asking people about a castle with certain characteristics, it is that it is a large castle with two towers, one of which is still standing, and the other is destroyed, and the answer was that the French countryside the area is teeming with old destructive castles and looks for him like a man looking for a needle in a haystack.

But this did not diminish Sarah's determination and did not discourage her from looking for her fiancé, and what pushed her was a dream, since her arrival in the village she dreamed over and over again, which increased her determination and determination.In the dream, some things began to change when she began to hear her fiance's voice urging her to come closer and that he was being held under the rubble and that he was waiting for her to find him.

Sarah walked long distances and it affected her when she lived on the alms of people who thought she was crazy, especially since her hair was disheveled and her clothes were shabby, and she moved from one village to another in search of her castle, and sleep does not leave her, and she still sees John every night in her dreams.

Until one day she reached an area with several castles, and when she saw one of them, she started screaming like crazy and rushed to her, she found the castle of her dreams!

She found a castle with two towers, one of which was destroyed, possibly by a shell, and found the wreckage just like in her dream. She rushed to her and began to remove the heavy stones with her weak hands. The villagers saw her and laughed at her, but some of them came forward to help her remove the stones, although they continued to mock them.

Until they heard a muffled cry from the rubble ...

The men froze in place when they heard a muffled sound, all except Sarah, who looked like a new force had arisen and was trying to remove the huge stones blocking the road.

Then a frantic campaign began and people gathered from nearby villages and formed a team to dig and remove the rubble to get to the prisoner under the rubble, and they could still hear his voice and the drilling continued all day until a hole covered in rubble was opened for them. , apparently the dome is in the past.

The men entered the dark cellar with caution, only to leave after a while, and in their arms, the shabby man showed his ribs clean that she could count, with a dusty beard, but Sarah knew him, he was John, her missing lover, ..

Sarah found her fiancé after losing a year and he was alive, although he could not see well because he lived in total darkness for a whole year.

After the situation calmed down and John's safety was confirmed, They asked him how he managed to survive a whole year without food or drink and how he managed to survive, Tell them that when the shell hit the tower, he fell into the old cellar of the castle, where wine and cheese were stored, and he could live on them for a whole year and felt his way to this, and his companions in his isolation were only rats.

Sarah and John returned to their home and were honorably discharged from the army and were honored and able to buy him a house after the end of the war and he married his girlfriend and his savior Sarah.

KELLY ANN BATES: THE GIRL LOVES STOLE HER EYES

Love is blind) Plato's famous proverb, Applies (Figuratively) Before it applies (Factually) Based on the story of a 17-year-old girl (Kelly Ann Bates) She was born on May 18, 1978, In Huttersley - UK, When her mindless love collided, as well as teenage Impulse, Sadism (James Patterson Smith) Fortieth man, With a dark past, About 30 years older than her.

You might think it's a common crime where a teenage girl fined a man older than her father and the story ended with the girl's death at the hands of her sadistic lover, but the details carry with it a heinous crime that chills her in the girl's life, this crime was known as his time (the most heinous crime in United Kingdom history).

James Patterson Smith: Wolf in Pregnancy

(Common man, divorced, Petotti, non-smoker, well-dressed, elegant and unemployed, lives in Gortana-Manchester - UK), so he knew him around him, but what was hidden from his personality was more than what he showed ,.

James was born in 1948 AD, sources do not mention his childhood or adolescence, which leads us to believe that he may have lived a normal life during these stages of his life, or at least a life far from the records of the authorities.

James) He was a man with several relationships, However, no official cases of violence were recorded in his record before he was killed (Kelly Ann) Only on three occasions, The first is his wife, This filed a divorce suit against him in 1980 after ten years of marriage, Due to excessive violence, And followed him the same year (Tina Watson) A twenty-year-old young woman, It was attracted by his quiet personality, I accepted him as a lover and lived with him for almost two years, not without violence from time to time, He even started using it as a boxing bag forever, Beating became a daily routine, she said, He went as far as to throw heavy metals or an ashtray on her head, He kicked her in the stomach while carrying her baby. And in the middle of 1982 AD, When he got tired of the relationship he decided to get rid of (Tina) I try to drown her while swimming, But the latter barely escaped and ran away.

Finally (Wendy Motherschild) 15 years old, who was also a victim of his violence and sadism, and she also escaped shortly after trying to drown her in the kitchen sink ..

Deadly coincidence: the beginning

There are people who can meet you with seashells, smile at them, and love them without even notifying you for a few seconds that they will be a curse that can happen to your life and end it in the blink of an eye, So it was a meeting (Kelly Ann) Damn her life (James) In early 1993 AD, When the seashells collected and met (James) Who was over 45 at the time, S (Kelly Ann) 14, She was known as an energetic girl with an old spirit, Because of her love to accompany those older than her, In the house of James's friend she was (Kelly Ann) She works as a nanny for her children for hours, A spark of love started at first sight between unequal parties.

Their relationship lasted two years, during which there were behavioral changes (Kelly Ann) And situations that raised doubts in her family that something had happened in their daughter's life, Once, she did not sleep (Kelly Ann) Sexually her at home the parents panicked, which made them call the police, For the first time, she didn't ask for their permission to stay overnight, But she came back the next morning saying that she spent the night at (Rachel's) her best friend, The next time, the girl came back with a big black bruise on the eye, She was attributed to the attack of a gang of girls who passed by, returning home, Thus, the little girl continued to extinguish her parents' suspicions in any situation, Until she finally decided to personally bring the cause of these doubts into the house to meet her mother's family. father and two brothers (Andrew) The biggest of them (Paul) Younger than her. As an introduction, and in order to prepare the family for the coming, the girl told them that the next visitor is her lover, who is 32 years old, which seemed wrong when I stepped (James) House for the first time, The big age difference was more than that what their daughter, Mama told them (Kelly this) She crossed, saying: (When I saw him, the chills hit me, I felt the bristles under my neck straight) Although the parents showed no reaction to the duo lying to them about Omar (James) At that time, However, they tried to convince (Kelly Ann) By moving away from him and not continuing in her relationship with him, And even severing her relationship with him forever, This increased the rebellion (Kelly Ann) And hold on to her lover, She spent most of their day at home.

In a Rapid Relationship: (Kelly Ann) left school and moved to James' home on Fernwal Gortan Street, and her family visits became rare, and each visit is a new stamp and new impact on the body of a 16-year-old girl at the time. .. Despite the obvious bruising and changes that accompanied her from a lot of weight loss and pallor in her face, (Kelly Ann) and in an attempt to cleanse her lover, she insisted that she was the result of accidents she was subjected to, like she was known as a sports girl who loved football and hockey.

But one night I decided to (Kelly Ann) Go back to her family's house after the disagreements and verbal squabbles between her and me (James) She also told her parents, A face filled with blue bruises, Then the mother decided to call the police and social services and file a complaint (James) But both sides refused to intervene without official communication (Kelly Ann) Personally, Ever since she came of age in UK law, Not to mention the victim initially refused to file a complaint against her lover, Or even admit at her level family that he caused these bruises.

Kill me and complain: the end

And in the chapter this is the last in her love story that she wrote with her own hand, Not knowing that this is the last chapter of her life, And I called it (Longing for a loved one) I decided (Kelly Ann) Return to her absent lover, Amidst the fear and her parents' reluctance and their warnings, especially after she confessed to them that she had to lie about Omar (James) So her family does not reject the relationship due to the big age difference between them.With her usual persistence and stubbornness, she fulfilled her wish and returned to him in November 1995.

In late December 1995, She resigned (Kelly Ann) From her job as a part-time mall, Her contact was almost permanently cut off from her family, Until mid-March 1996, when she sent her parents a birthday card on the occasion of their wedding anniversary, Then the family noticed that the line on the card was not their daughter's line, Which prompted the brother (Kelly it), (Andrew) To visit her in Gortana, Then it was impossible (James) She went shopping and will be late, And it seems that her brother was convinced of this argument and returned from the place where he had come without calming down, But her mother, despite her concern about the illness of her youngest son (Pavel) And the hernia operation performed by the young during this period, She could communicate on the phone with her daughter, who seemed calm and unnatural (According to the mother) And with (James) Around.

On the evening of April 17, 1996 A.D., James went to the police station, claiming that his beloved died of suffocation from the bath water in his house after a fight, and there was an argument between them, and that he tried to revive her, but his attempt was not crowned with success. The police immediately went to the house (James) Based on his communication, There, the police were surprised to find the body of (Kelly Ann) Naked in the master bedroom with no eyes, In addition to the huge number of wounds and bruises in her body, The remains of her hair on the heating pipes at home showed that he attached her hair to a heating beam (Assuming the human body is at least 1 cm away from him) Blood was also observed in all rooms and around the house, The police described the scene as (The most horrible scene and the worst crime in their practical history in terms of the gruesome deformation of the body and the hideous places of torture) Which proved to them that the accident is much more than drowning, Accordingly, he was arrested (James).

True Tragedy: Anatomy

In my professional history, I have examined about 600 murder victims, But I have not seen horrible, brutal and pervasive wounds like these in Kelly Ann Bates's body) This is what the anatomy doctor in charge of the case said (Kelly Ann) Doctor

(William Lawler) He stated that the victim lived almost three weeks before his death without eyes, After he got up (James) Pulling her eyes out with his hands, And without food or water for at least five days, And she spent almost a month under physical torture, Real the tragedy experienced by the victim before her death, where she died and her body bore more than 150 wounds, in detail as follows:

The thigh burns when eaten hot.

Burns on some parts of the body with hot water.

Broken arm.

Puncture wounds are spread throughout the body using various sharp machines, in particular: knives, food forks, scissors.

Puncture wounds in the mouth and face.

- break the bones of the hands.

- Break the knee bones.

Distorted wounds in the ears, eyebrows, nose and lips.

- Rupture and complete rupture of the genitals.

Various wounds with a dirty shovel and tree pruning shears.

Rooting out her eyes with his hands and stabbing empty quarries with a knife.

Partial skin of the scalp.

Unfair stab wounds to her buttocks and left leg.

- A strong blow to the head with a hard tool.

Doctor. Lawler added that any of these injuries, despite their depth, inflammation and brutality, were not the main cause of Kelly Ann's death, which was due to drowning.

Confession without regret (challenge me): Judgment

Insist (James) He is not guilty of willful murder and only confesses to torture, Sticking to the story of a previous drowning, After pressure from the authorities and confronting the autopsy results (Kelly Ann) I admit he hit her in the head with a bathtub that caused her to pass out before drowning her, he added that she provoked him to harm her until she insulted his late mother, and that the victim hurt herself until she accused him, In conclusion, when the investigator responsible for the cause of his perseverance to such an extent that he rips out her eyes and stabs empty careers, he replied: she challenged me !!.

- The prosecutor in the case (Peter Open Show) He said in his request: (The injuries and wounds on the victim's body were not the result of sudden emotions or haste to react, Rather, it seemed that he deliberately disfigured and slowly hurt her and insulted her dignity, And for a long period of time, There was no part of her body without a tone, Her death was undoubtedly a merciful end to her torment).

"With regard to the psychological report, he indicated that (James) was suffering from paranoia and deadly jealousy, but this did not belong to the category of psychiatric patients whose condition required imprisonment in special centers.

- It took a jury less than an hour to judge (James) 49 years old, guilty of murder (Kelly Ann Bates) and torture, after seeing photographs of the victim, which the court used by a psychological counselor to help the jury deal with the violent and heinous crimes of the picture. (Pictures of Kelly Ann after her death were never shown due to her disgrace).

During the trial, Judge (Judge Sachs) commented: (This is a terrible case of abuse and skewing of one person over another, you are a very dangerous person, offending women, and I intend and as long as the power is in my hands at the present time, don't let you repeat your crime again.) And he was sentenced to life in prison with no parole 25 years ago.

THE LOVE THAT CLOSED THE MOUNTAIN

There are many strange and miracles in India, perhaps the most famous and most memorable of them is the Taj Mahal temple, which was chosen several years ago as the miracle of the Seven Wonders of the New World, and the Taj Mahal for those who do not know it is the majestic temple built by the Mughal Emperor Shah Jahan in memory of his late wife, Mumtaz Mahal, who was a great love for her, so that his design perfectly influenced the fate of this love, and they rejoiced in its magnificence with a story of sincerity and loyalty that united the spouses, It is no wonder that after that tourists come to him from different parts of the earth to break their eyes upon seeing its walls and white ivory domes.

But what most people don't know is that India includes another masterpiece similar to the Taj Mahal in terms of meaning and significance, just like another man who loved his wife so much and wanted to perpetuate her memory indelibly a building that punishes days and years, it is true that this is not a wonderful Taj Mahal, It does not match it in terms of precision of workmanship and exquisite appearance, but it is no less fair in terms of greatness of achievement, given its modest potential creator, as he was not an authority, nor rich, and did not possess a footnote, servants and decency, but rather a simple man, called "Dashrat Manji", did not belong to the horoscope of the world and its decoration, except for a modest hut, a rusty old ax, and four thin sheep .. But he was not as poor as you think, and consider my dear reader, because the poor is the one who compares himself to others and becomes sad because he does not have what they have. As for the rich, it is content that only looks at his hands, he is satisfied with his livelihood and buys peace of mind for little money. Our friend was of the latter type, pleased with what the Lord brought him, I am not complaining or complaining, but rather to see how he explains his chest, always smiling, and this question became a reason for the surprise of his neighbors and colleagues in the coal mine in which he works because he is the poorest of them all, and the least of them is because he belongs to the untouchable class that lies at the bottom of the Hindu caste .. Still, he is happy, happy, so what is his secret? ..

In fact, there was no secret. It was very simple. Our friend possessed wealth that others rarely possessed, not gold, diamonds or rubies, but a good, beautiful, loyal and persuasive wife, and most of all interested in the comfort of her husband and children, so she was the source of his happiness, and the secret of his happiness And the light in which his eyes are broken.

But one of the facts of a bitter life is that nothing lasts in it, because everything has a conclusion and an end, even the happiness of our friend "Dashrat" for its simplicity and smallness. One day, "Dashrat" went to work in a mine on the outskirts of his city, where there are mountains and rocky hills, and his wife used to bring him food and water every day at lunchtime, and while she was on the way to this, clay the vessels slipped when she slid her foot down one of the slopes. She rolled down the slope, was seriously injured, and people carried her to her house, bleeding.

When Dashrat returned from his work, he was surprised by his wife, who was bedridden and thickened by a surgeon who was in poor condition and had to be immediately transferred to a hospital for treatment, but there is a high mountain that divides the small town of Galur. where Dashrat lives and the big city where the hospital is located, and turn into a mountain I had to walk in stormy metaphors at a distance of 70 km, and accordingly, an ambulance could not arrive, my wife could not be transferred, and she soon breathed the next day.

The death of his beloved wife was a great shock, which shook the essence of "Dashrat" and turned his life upside down, so he drowned in deep sadness, and he stayed in his house, cut off from people, and he remained so for several days, barely eating or drinking and spends time crying..

But one morning the neighbors were surprised that "Dashrat" came out of his house with a bushy beard, curling his hair, carrying his ax on his shoulder and heading towards the mountain that separates the city from the big city, and when they asked him: Where are you going? .. He answered them, saying that he was going to teach grief a lesson, because he prevented the ambulance of his wife and caused her death! .. They shook their heads, regretting the man, and thought that he had gone insane because of the shock of his wife's death.

But Dashrat was not as crazy as they thought, he had a plan, maybe a little crazy! But in the end, this is an idea that he believed in and worked to bring it to fruition at any cost. The man wanted to get into the heart of the mountain in order to connect his remote city with a big city where there are hospitals, schools, government offices and jobs .. He said that he did not want another woman to suffer the same fate as his wife, because that she cannot be taken to the hospital, and does not want the children of his city to be left without education due to the inaccessibility of schools, and does not want her youth to remain unemployed due to their inability to get a job .. The road that Dashrat planned to build in the heart mountains, would reduce the distance to the city from only 70 km to 15 km and make it easier for people to access hospitals, schools and jobs in the city.

Of course, Samia and Nabila were the targets of "Dashrat", but this also seemed impossible in every respect. No wonder this man has become a laughing stock for his city, a place of ridicule and a lack of his people, how can a skinny and poor man who has only a rusty ax break into the heart of a mountain? .. However, the irony did not prevent Dashrat from continuing his project, but rather strengthened his will and determination, so he sold his four wards to buy at the price of the psalms that hit the stone ..

Days, months and years went by, and Dashrat went up the mountain every evening to work on the road, while the day was spent plowing others' fields to get some money to support his children and his family.

Gradually, that small hole that Dashrat made at the top of the mountain turned into a big hole, and the hole turned into an abyss, and the abyss - into a large cut .. And the laughter and sarcasm of people turned with her into surprise, surprise and charm, and some of them brought food to Dashrat, while others supplied him with chisels and hammers ..

In the end, the pipe dream turned into reality, "Dashrat" managed to close the mountain and split its rocky heart eight meters deep and 110 meters long. But it was not easy and it was not achieved overnight. Rather, it has taken 22 years of continuous hard work since Dashrat started in 1960 and graduated in 1983.

So the person they said about him is insane and they turned his poverty and poverty and looked worse at him .. He became a national myth, a miracle of India, and became a role model for altruism and sacrifice for the common good.

Dashrat Manji died in 2007 ... The "Mountain Man" is gone, as he was called, but his mountain still remains, and he will forever tell the world a story about a man whose only heart beats with love and an iron will to turn the impossible into reality.

CHINESE CASANOVA: HOW DO YOU GET 18 MISTRESSES ?!

Yuan Mo is a Chinese civil engineer from Changsha, Hunan Province, China.

On April 1, 2015, Yuan Mu was in a car accident, passed out and made people happy in the hospital.

Hospital staff did not find a way to contact Yuan's family to inform them of what had happened, so they called the last numbers Yuan had given before the accident.

Which was registered on his mobile phone with strange symbols!

Unfortunately, none of the numbers they named was the Yuan family number. After these calls, a group of women in their 20s and 40s began arriving at Yuan's hospital ward to check on him, and each of them was surprised when she came with the others.

Engineer Yuan was a big crook, as the final number of his visitors at the hospital was 17 women, each of whom was considered his only lover and his future wife.

Some of these women began their relationship with Yuan over 10 years ago, until he became a father to one of them and planned to marry another, in addition to promising them all to marry.

None of them thought that the strange characters on Yuan's phone were hidden behind the numbers of his other mistresses, because he deceived each of them that they were his colleagues' numbers.

18 months ago, Shao Li, who was Yuan's mistress, said, (I was very afraid and cried a lot when they told me that he had an accident, but when I saw many good deeds coming to the hospital to check on him, I could not keep crying. The same lie lied to us.).

After this incident, Yuan's former mistresses formed a group to talk about an application (WeChat) they called (Alliance for Revenge), and through the talks between them on that group, it became clear that Yuan was asking 17 mistresses for money every month.

Chinese police arrested engineer Yuan for cheating on his mistresses and taking money from them by deceiving them, so that it would be clear during the investigation that he had not only cheated women.

Investigators found that Yuan earned a degree in civil engineering from a respected university called (South Central) in order to be able to find work even if he actually got a high school diploma!

- JEAN DE LESS .. VENGEFUL PIRATE.

In 1300, a child named (Jan de Belleville) was born in a French city called (Belleville Sur V).

Gene's father was the sole heir to the wealthy De Belleville family, who had lived in the area for hundreds of years. Jan's father died when she was three years old, leaving a legacy to her entire family.

At the age of twelve, Jan married a nineteen-year-old named (Geoffrey de Chateauprent), Geoffrey was a noble Brittany, and also inherited many estates from his family.

Ian's marriage to Geoffrey was an ordinary marriage, and this marriage ended with Geoffrey's death in 1326.

Two years after his death in 1328, she remarried to Jean, but this time her marriage did not last long because Pope John XXII canceled this marriage.

1330.

In the same year she married Jean for the third time, this time she married a man named (Olivier de Clison IV), who is also a noble Brittany and very rich, but this time the marriage was very different for Jean.

Olivier was about the same age as Jan and was also a widow. Therefore, they were very appropriate as a couple. Their marriage was based not only on understanding, but also on a real race of love between them. Jean-Olivier gave birth to five children

Isabo - Maurice - Jean - Olivier V - Guillaume

Unfortunately, the happiness of Jan and her husband did not last long, in 1341 a war broke out between France and England in Brittany, and Olivier took part in this war.

In addition to the Duke of Brittany (Charles de Blois), supported by (Philip VI) the King of France in November 1342.

Olivier was with a group of noble lords in the city of Van in the Brittany region, who defended the city from successive attacks by the British.

After four unsuccessful attempts, the British managed to storm the city, and Olivier was captured by the British, just two months after this incident, in particular on January 19, 1343, an armistice was signed between England and France (malstroit), and Olivier was released with ransom.

It didn't matter (Charles de Blois) Duke of Brittany because he was suspected of plotting to fall the city of Van, he suspected that the men did not defend it enough, and when the British demanded a small amount of money as ransom to free Olivier, Doubts Charles's betrayal and surrender of the city to the British was strengthened by Olivier and the nobles who were with him.

Olivier was invited with the fifteen noble lords of Brittany who were in the city of Van when she fell to celebrate the truce, and during the ceremony they were arrested and taken to Paris, and despite the absence of any evidence of their betrayal, they were executed by beheading. August 2, 1343 and without any trial.

Olivier's body was suspended in Paris, and his head was sent to Nantes to hang there.

When the news reached Jean, she became very angry and vowed to avenge her husband from the Duke of Brittany (Charles de Blois) and from (Felipe VI) the King of France.

Jan took his two sons (Guillaume) and (Olivier V) to Nantes to see their father's head and told them that the king of France and (Charles de Blois) had killed him.

After that, she returned to her city and sold all the land and property that could be sold, and a group of her faithful husband's followers and other noble followers who were executed and sympathizers gathered around her.

I went with these people to visit the castle of a man named (Galois de Laheus) It was (Gallois) Sincerely (Charles de Blois) But the news of Olivier's execution has not yet arrived, so Jan received in his castle, Jan and her people turned on (Gallois) They killed most of his garrisons and forced several of them to tell what happened.

Jan took everything of value from the castle and left with her people.

After that, she bought three warships with her own money and prepared them, and went with her black fleet to the Magny Sea, which separates France from England.

For forty-three years Yang stood on the deck of the main ship, which she named (re), to act as a pirate against merchant ships carrying the French flag.

Yang began hunting French ships, and every time she ordered her men to kill most of the ship's crew, they brutally attacked and left a few survivors to tell the story and break the news to the King of France.

The nobles in her hands suffered more than others, and despite the opportunity to receive a large ransom in exchange for their release, Yang decapitated himself with an ax before throwing his bodies into the sea, Jan's strength earned her the title (Brittany lion).

Jan's revenge was not only about piracy, but his ships crossed the Manch Sea, carrying supplies from the English army, as it also attacked some coastal villages in Normandy, and as an expression of their gratitude, the British provided them with land in the areas they controlled in Brittany.

Although King Philip died in 1350, Jean did not stop his campaign against the French.

In one of the battles off the French coast, Jan's ship sank, her son Guillaume died, and Jan and her son Olivier disappeared.

They were found and rescued five days later by the British in Brittany.

After the death of her son, she left the life of pirates and ended her 13-year campaign against the French.

In 1356 she married Jan for the fourth time, married an English lord named (Walter Bentley), who is one of the military deputies of the King of England (Edward III).

Jan spent the rest of her life in a castle overlooking the sea on the southern coast of Brittany and died in peace in 1359.

After Jan's death, her family's legacy lasted a long time, her son Olivier went to war in Brittany against an old family enemy (Charles de Blois) in the battle (Uraj), where Charles finally died. Olivier lost his eye in this battle and later became known as the "butcher".

With the death of Charles, Olivier took revenge on his father, and then made peace with the French.

By 1380, Olivier was appointed to what was then called (policeman of France) and this seems to be the name of a modest position, but this position actually means that he was the main nobleman or prime minister in the kingdom, that is, the second person in power and authority right after the king.

When Olivier died in 1407, he was the richest man in France, and even the king (Francis I), who became king of France in 1515, was a descendant of Olivier.

That is, the blood of Jean (the lioness of Brittany) and her husband Olivier, who took revenge on him, ran with the blood of

MOUSTAFA ABDELGAUAD

French kings from 1515 to 1848

PEDRO I: THE KING WHO LOVES TURNED INTO A MONSTER

That is why I decided today to enrich your information with a story about Portugal and its history, about the king of its kings, whom people called "cruel" for his blood and the severity of his punishment, but in fact he was not cruel throughout his life, like cruelty is not necessarily part of human nature and instinct, but can be acquired as a result of a bitter experience or a shock earthquake, and this is exactly what happened to the hero of our story, how he had a pure heart, overflowing with love and tenderness, but they stepped on him heart, crushed it, and turned it into a monster that knows no mercy.

Let's not prolong the conversation, come with me to go straight to the royal palace in Lisbon and enter the throne room where King Alfonso IV of Portugal sat on his majestic throne, his face was red and his wounds were swollen as he looked at his son and the heir to his throne, Prince Pedro, who bowed at his father's feet with indulgence and humiliation, and was not in the hall, except for them, two guards stood like two idols motionless at the entrance to the hall.

Prince Pedro said in a tone, please, straight with his head: "Please, dad .. Don't force me to do what I don't want. ".

And the king shouted at him, saying: "You must marry her .. do not argue with me .. This is an order. ".

The prince stood up and said, condemning: "How can I marry her for God's sake?" .. This woman was the ex-wife of my sister's husband! ".

"So he broke off his marriage and is now available." .. The king said to argue.

"But why did Donna insist on this woman for all the women of the earth, Dad?" The prince said, interesting.

- "I want to teach him a lesson .. This bastard is your sister's husband .. Alfonso XI .. Our spies say that he mistreats my daughter and publicly accepts mistresses, besides her father, with her feelings and dignity, although she gave birth him as heir to the throne. ".. And don't forget that her father is one of the noblest and most powerful." .. It's a good idea to win him with us in any future fight against your sister's stupid husband. ".

- I don't like this woman, dad .. Please excuse me from this marriage. ".. The prince said with a tone of begging.

- "I cannot return to my opinion, and you know it well .. This marriage will take place, even if, despite your nose. ".. The king said, emphasizing, then he got up from his throne in harmony and turned back to enter through a small door covered with a red curtain, located directly behind the throne, and the prince was left alone in the hall, and he walked walking with the wind and coming, clapping his hands with regret and sadness, not knowing what to do to convince the father to give up this marriage.

And what a strict father wanted, since Prince Pedro Margma married Princess Constance, the ex-wife of King Alfonso XI of Castile (Spain). The bride came from Castile to Portugal to meet her groom, not only, of course, but also with an army of servants and bridesmaids ..

There is no doubt that such a husband, based on interests and whims, would not bear love and happiness, so that Prince Pedro's heart never failed his bride, it is true that they were connected with the marriage charter, and together they had three children, but the prince never loved her, but his heart was suspended, ironically.One of her bridesmaids that she brought with her from Castile, Ennis de Castro, is a beautiful girl with wide blue eyes, and her skin is so white that historians have said, that sitting in front of her, you can see red wine flowing through her neck when she sips it! ..

Ennis traded the prince for love, and it was not normal love, but explosives and a bonfire, and it didn't take long until their relationship became in every language throughout the kingdom, which made Constance's heart hate her beautiful summer, banish her from court and order her to return immediately to Castile, but Prince Pedro intervened and took his mistress to live with him in one of his palaces.

In fact, it wasn't weird at the time that kings and princes would take boyfriends and mistresses for their wives, so King Alfonso IV initially didn't mind his son's relationship with the runner-up who thought it was a temporary one-to-one relationship, a fleeting whim. but the days soon proved his mistake .. His spies began to convey to him disturbing news of the growing influence of the Ennis brothers on Prince Pedro, and he brought them in and appointed them to prestigious positions and made them the subject of his secret, and his advisers take their opinion as a big and in the little one that raised the king's anger and angered the Portuguese nobles, since relations between Portugal and Castile were often tense and based on competition and power struggles, and no one in Portugal would, of course, want to see how the prince of the country and the heir to the throne becomes a play in the hands of a group of Castilians.

King Alfonso began to insist that his son break off relations with Ennis, but the prince stubbornly refused. Fate wanted Constance to die after the birth of her third child in 1345, describing the atmosphere for lovers, and decided to marry, but this was met with categorical refusal and outrage from the king and nobles, since how can the heir to the throne of Portugal marry the runner-up ... Not all of Prince Pedro's pleas and intercessions made his father change his mind, and between them things got worse until the boycott reached the point. The king's anger and resentment increased Pedro's superb interest in his illegitimate children from his mistress in exchange for his neglect of his royal children from his wife Constance.

In conclusion, the king decided to put an end to all this, and he was determined to kill Ennis, and when he showed the case to his entourage, three nobles volunteered to finish it, and Prince Pedro hid him with his children in the monastery, fearing her from his father, but the king's spies discovered her place, so three nobles set off on a sinister night since 1355 to the monastery and secretly entered Ennis's room while Prince Pedro was away, they killed her, cut her head in front of their children's eyes, and took him to the king.

When Prince Pedro returned to examine Ennis, he found her dead body and saw his children crying with dismay and anxiety .. He lost his mind .. He was determined to take revenge, even if it cost him his life .. Soon he collected army and declared war on his father, and a bloody brutal war broke out between the two sides, the victorious king was in this, but not for long, when death suddenly raided him as a result of illness, and Pedor was crowned king of Portugal under the name of King Pedro I.

The first thing Pedro did when he took the throne was to avenge Ennis' death, so he sent his men to look under each rock and the three nobles who killed Ennis, and two of them were arrested, while the third managed to escape and hide in Castile.

According to historians, King Pedro killed two men as killers in disguise in an innovative way, as their hearts reached out with living hands, he took the first's heart from the front through the chest, while he removed the second's heart from the back through the back, and it was said that he did it is with them because of the pain and pain that caused him to kill their Linness.

The second strange thing that Bidur did after his coronation as king was that he collected the celebrities, nobles and nobles of Portugal, then removed Ennis's body from her grave, put her head back to her body, dressed her as a queens, and sat on the throne next to him, then asked everyone to come one by one to kiss her hand and sell it to her as queen. Thus, the runner-up who condemned their queen while she was alive became a rotting corpse! .. Bedor ruled for another ten years before he died, and before he died, he ordered to build two very beautiful graves in one of the cathedrals, one for Linis, and another for him, and he made them able to meet each other , and wrote between them on marble the phrase: "together until the end of the world."

MARRIAGE FROM ANOTHER WORLD

Marriage is that sacred bond that all societies respect with different cultures and customs. When the newlyweds stand and vow to be good and bad together until death do them part, this does not mean that death is the end of this relationship, where Hindus believe that marriage is an eternal bond that continues for seven more lifetimes. This is why the groom's turban party is associated with the bride's party, and the couple swims around the fire seven times and vows to live together in the next, seven lives, and there are strange rituals all over the world that the article cannot accommodate, but like a marriage when one of the two parties from another world ?, Is this dark world dominated by souls and ghosts?

In the state of Haiti, this island is located in the Caribbean, whose inhabitants are famous for the practice of voodoo magic, this is magic based on the use of evil spirits by marrying a person and these dark entities in a way similar to signing a contract with Satan, where they fulfill the wishes of this person, in return he committed this man by offering offerings and sex with these demons.

In Haiti, this perfume is called Lwa, and this spiritual marriage takes place on Saturday night, where offerings are prepared, which are usually made from jewelry and perfume, and the priest of the village lights a fire and throws incense, and during this smoke the next man or woman will get married. for this marriage in his curly white outfit, he lies on the ground adorned with symbols and magic talismans, then the drums are knocked out and Zagared is pushed off the lips of the rest of the tribe. Meanwhile, the groom trembles, a strong vibration, and writhes like a serpentine bullfight, where it is believed that the spirit of the Dambala snake has captured him, then the priest feeds him a boiled egg, which the person completely eats with his skin, like a snake, and then he stops trembling. and then the priest orders one of the girls to dance with him until the spirit puts on him and the marriage takes place without sexual contact.

And in case the lying woman is a woman, the man is forced to dance with her until the soul wears it, because in the end she is just a soul and needs a human body, and after this dance everyone leaves, and the marriage took place without sexual contact. and according to the agreement that the spirit realizes the desires that her husband asks for her in exchange for that husband who sleeps with her one night a month up to 3 nights a week, and during this period he has no right to approach a human woman, otherwise he angered this spirit and caused sickness, poverty and madness in it.

As for how this husband spends his night with this spirit, after the husband wears a dress in the color that the spirit loves, wears rings, lies on a special bed and sleeps on it. During sleep, this spirit comes in the form of a brown woman who wears a crown on her head and has a spiritual connection with what is happening. It resembles physical euphoria, after which a man is exhausted by the benevolence of strength. Haitian priests believe that these devilish spirits are called Erzuli, a demonic spirit requested by Haitian witches of African descent, and are embodied in the form of a brown woman who wears a crown on her head and is adorned with golden flowers of various colors. And the pleasant scent has three rings in her hand and they are called Dampala, Hello and Ojon, and these are the names of her husbands, and this symbolizes her in the shape of a heart and is homosexual sexual orientation, as itself the embodiment of two sisters in the shape of twins.

The first sister's name is Erzuli Frida, she loves men and prefers pink, blue, white and yellow, and the priests approach her with rings, jewelry, gold, perfume, alcoholic drinks, and sweet cakes with sugar, and when she accepts this offer, she is wearing her husband, and he quickly takes this for an offer. After the wedding ceremony, Erzuli Farida promises her husband to fulfill his material needs, such as money and other things. As for the other sister, her name is Erzuli Dantors.

And this is different from her first sister with two scratches on her face, and she loves children and women, and her favorite colors are black, red and blue and pigs are killed as offerings for her, and she loves blood, and for this the husband cuts himself with a knife seven times to satisfy her, and unlike her sister is unique, how this spirit meets spiritual demands such as magic works, and she is very jealous and does not tolerate those who betray her.

Of course, these are not just myths and tribal heritage, but real magic, which is considered one of the foundations of voodoo magic.

Japan has a less scary charm than the magic of Haiti, and it carries with it something romantic and loyal to parents to their dead children. After the end of World War II, Japan lost the war, and the killing of hundreds of thousands of soldiers and civilians, the mothers of the dead soldiers were very upset about their children, who were killed in their prime and did not marry, It is said that a Japanese woman communicated with the spirit of her deceased son during a session to prepare life and told her that he was stuck in the world of souls and that he needed someone to comfort his unit, and when she told the priests to do this, they suggested that she make a little doll in the form of a girl, dressed in the clothes of the bride, and takes her to one of the temples. There, the soul of her son will be married to this doll until his soul is at peace. This doll is called the bride of Hanayome ningyo

Indeed, this woman performed the marriage ceremony at the Kobuji temple, and from that day on, the temple received a huge number of dolls from mothers who lost their children in this war.

Kobuji Temple is located in Tsugaru City, Omori Province, northern Japan, and one of the monks of Kobuji Temple says: the temple contains more than 900 glass containers with dolls in the form of bride and groom, which contained photographs of dead sons and several pieces pirogue

Initially, several dolls arrived at the temple, and after a reporter visited one of the TV channels in the temple in the eighties and made a press coverage of the temple, the temple was very famous and the number of dolls reaching the temple increased to ten dolls a day and people moved from sending cheap dolls for hands to buy well-made and expensive dolls for the happiness of their deceased children, but now only 3 dolls a year from parents who lost their children due to traffic accidents or suicides arrived at the temple, and precious dolls have become very rare, although the monks in this temple continue to make sure that the dolls pray for the souls of the dead so that they can enjoy peace in another world

Although talk about death is terrifying in the soul, there is a posthumous marriage or what is called necrogamy, and this marriage is different from necrophilia, in which people have sexual relations with corpses, nikrogs are a virgin relationship between a living person and his deceased lover. France is one of the few countries to have passed this law, and the date it was passed is linked to a strange incident that took place in France.

On December 2, 1959, the Malbasit Dam, located in the south of France, collapsed and caused torrential floods that engulfed the village of Frijos, resulting in 423 deaths and huge material losses estimated at 68 million. President Charles de Gaulle traveled to the village of Frichos to view the aftermath of the destruction and to offer condolences to the victims of the flood during his visit, the President of France met a girl named Irene Goddart, who begged him and tears flowed from her eyes and asked him to allow her to end her marriage with her fiancé Andre Cabra, who died in the flood, it was a shock for President de Gaulle, who promised her to pass a law for this, and with the sympathy of the population And pressure from the media on Irina's case, Parliament adopted a law on marrying the living from the dead, since this marriage and what obligations are followed?

This marriage occurs after a man or woman has come to court to ask for marriage to his deceased lover, and the court reviews the request and must provide witnesses and evidence that they wanted to marry before death parted them and after how the court agreed that this marriage is celebrated, and the bride stands apart from her beloved, imprisoned in a coffin and receiving marriage vows, but without mentioning the sentence to death divides us, because the husband is basically dead, and after the wedding the wife is called a widow, but she has no right to claim inheritance or acquire the citizenship of a deceased husband, since the purpose of the legislation of this marriage is to preserve romance among loved ones whose death separated them before they got married, as well as to attribute children to their parents who died before marriage.

In some African regions, it is believed that the marriage ceremony for divorced and married couples should be performed in an unconventional manner before being buried, and an African priest says that death is simply the separation of the soul from the body and the beginning of another life.

In the state of Ebony, in southeastern Nigeria, a very strange accident has occurred. After Margaret Emmanuelle placed her two twins in the city hospital, she died after complications in childbirth. It shocked her husband, Adigo Emmanuel, a poor 50-year-old who had just lost his wife and took charge of caring for this twins in addition to his four children. And amid accumulating debt, Emmanuel decided to bury his wife, perhaps he forgets something about his tragedy to be surprised at the ban on her funeral by her family, who insisted that he hold a wedding for his deceased daughter because they do not recognize church marriage. This was a problem for Emmanuel, as he does not mind this tradition, but he does not have the cost of the celebration, estimated at a thousand dollars.

In 2004, a gruesome crime took place in the small village of Ceres in South Africa when a violent altercation occurred between David McInta and his fiancée, Mugania Mulomo. When the quarrel intensified, David decided to resolve the situation and shot his pregnant bride with his child, and he wanted her dead, and when David felt the gravity of his crime, he raised his gun and fired a bullet from it, which penetrated his head to commit suicide. The strange thing is that the family of the two victims decided to hold a wedding ceremony for them, and the wedding ceremony took place in the presence of two bodies, which were adorned with wedding clothes amid the joy of those present.

Looking for a bride for the deceased in China

And there is a kind of horrific romance in China where the Chinese believe that single boys who die at the age of 14 and into their teens and older do not enjoy the comforts of the afterlife and will return to haunt their families and cause them bad luck, so parents must search for the body of a lonely girl who recently died and is buried next to the body of this young man until his soul relaxes, this weather is very old and dates back to the 17th century BC, but, with Chinese leader Mao Zedong taking office in 1949 year, he passed a law criminalizing those who rebel with this two-year prison sentence, but some Chinese families still practice this weather in rural northern China and pay exorbitant sums to buy the bodies of single girls where wealthy families buy bodies. from hospitals and brokers, complete the deal and give them a body with contract paper to burn later over the grave, like a kind of pony for the newlywed in.

As for middle-aged families, they buy bodies from grave robbers who dig graves and steal the bodies of girls, and the price of the body depends on its condition. More recent and not rotten, the higher the price and the price can reach 20 thousand dollars, and in 2013 the police made the Chinese arrested four people in the Shaanxi area from grave robbers, and they admitted that they had exhumed 10 graves and sold the bodies of girls for 40,000 dollars ... The funny thing is that grave robbers steal the bodies again after selling them to sell them again, and this could have been agreed between the two families, as happened in February 2012 when a poor Chinese family sold the body of their late daughter to a wealthy family for £ 3,700.

But the law criminalizes these acts for fear of committing crimes to obtain these organs, and Chinese newspapers wrote about the crime that took place in northwest China in April

2016, and details were revealed when police arrested three people when they smuggled the body of a woman in their car, and after criminal interrogation, analysis showed that the woman was poisoned during the investigation of the leader of a gang called Ma Chung Hwa, 60, where he admitted that he had lured one woman with special needs who was over forty years old, lured her to her fiance, and then lured her to his apartment in the Gansu district, where he killed her with a poisonous injection that she would not show the effect of violence on her body and would sell her body, and ten days later he committed his second crime and killed one woman in aged 60, but police arrested him while transporting a body to sell to his two assistants.

As for poor families who have no money, they buy decomposed bodies at a low price to complete the wedding ceremony, or they only make bridesmaid cakes and put them on the grave of their late son.

VOYEUR

Imagine going on vacation and staying at a hotel and find that all of your movements and living conditions are monitored and literally studied ... To completely lose your privacy and be under the eyes of a person who loves to watch people ..

This is what Gerald Voss, the human freak, was doing, a habit that reached his addiction stage .. This habit originated in Voss in early childhood when he sat in his garden, hoping to cross with passion ..

At the age of twenty, his aunt moved to the next house, and Voss found her an interesting opportunity to satisfy his curiosity and watched her daily from behind a glass.

Voss enjoyed seeing people naked or having sex, and to satisfy his observation instinct, which increased over time, he bought the manor and added a hidden loft shelf in all hotel rooms. Voss built this hidden shelf with the help of his wife to avoid raising suspicion. His wife shared voyeurism! They sometimes felt euphoric while having sex together on a hidden shelf above the prisoners' heads! ..

Voss's journey began to observe prisoners only without interference, he loved nudity and sex, patient hours on this dark shelf to get an injection .. But he hated drug addicts and drug dealers, so he took the opportunity to stay out of his rooms and get rid of drugs , which once led to murder, as the guest killed his partner, thinking that she took the drug alone .. The strange thing is that Voss watched this issue and did not move his finger, and later said that he thought that the girl had only passed out and did not know that she died until the next day when the worker found the body.

Voss also hated the prisoners who owned pets, especially the dog, because she sensed his presence, smelled his scent, and would not stop barking when he crawled into his hidden place.

Voss was not satisfied with the observation .. Sometimes he left some pornographic magazines inside the rooms to see the reaction of the prisoners, or perhaps change them with sex, and some of them urged to object to the existence of these things, and some of them accepted their existence.

Voss had the strange conviction that he was a researcher of the human psyche and that his voyeurism was not an aberration, but a scientific study! .. From the very beginning of his founding at the Manor House he had many notebooks detailing the various guests, their nature and habits, even their weight, length and skin color .. The bottom line is that Voss considered himself a scientist, not a voyeur, and he viewed what he did as a sacrifice in order to understand the human psyche and its sexual behavior, especially since he spent most of his life in this research (approximately twenty-five years) since the sixties. century.

Journalist Jay Teles once met Voss and the friendship between them was fortified to the point that Voss told him what he was doing to steal his hotel guests.Not only that, He even accompanied him on his voyeur tours.He almost found out. when Teles' tie fell off one of the vents, so Foss pulled it quickly before the inhabitants of the room hinted at it ..

As a result of the friendship developed between Voss and Teles, Voss passed on his observation books to Teles.

It is strange that Teles did not disclose Voss's perverse hobby, citing Voss forcing him to sign a newspaper so as not to publish any information about him if Voss did not allow it, which some consider journalistic betrayal.

Teles' friendship with Voss continued until he finished writing a book about him called (Snoopy), and episodes of the same name were released on Netflix in 2013. For your information, renowned American filmmaker Steven Spielberg bought the rights to the novel and wanted to turn it into a film, but he changed his mind after the novel was filmed.

Finally, the reader may ask .. How is a person who confesses to voyeurism and violates their privacy, and a novel has been written about him, and he is still free and free, not arrested by the police and not even interrogated ?! ..

The answer is that Voss has stopped voyeurism, as he claims since 1996, and therefore the statute of limitations.This is because many years have passed since the crime.Moreover, no one has filed a complaint against him.In conclusion, the only evidence in the case, the Manor House Hotel was demolished and its aftermath wiped out .. So there's nothing to blame Voss .. He'll probably remain a free road that openly boasts a voyeur for years.

Pay attention to the nightmare site: Voyeurism is classified as a type of sexual deviation, especially when it turns into a habit and addiction, and is punished by law and law .. Unfortunately, these voyeurs are not few. How many of a noble man have been struck by God by a bad neighbor who sneaks behind a curtain or on top of a balcony and surfaces.

A STORY OF ADORATION THAT HAS BEEN GOING ON FOR MORE THAN HALF A CENTURY !!!

Is true and true love available? That love, whose spark does not go out and does not depend on the time factor? This is the love that our hero felt for each other. The events of our history took place in Russia in the mid-twenties of the twentieth century during the rule of Stalin, who was known for his cruelty to the point that he called him by nicknames such as "Iron Man", where his authoritarian policies killed millions of his citizens, scattered and deprived families.

Today Anna Kozlov is an elderly woman, laid on her head with fine white hair, interspersed with spaces to show her scalp. Barely walking and contemplating the streets of Provilitsa, Siberia .. From time to time she stands to catch her breath and wipe her wrinkled face with a Balinese handkerchief, which removed it from the folds of her dress. The old man in his car caught her with great effort. Anna froze in her place and for a while thought that she was imagining ... The old man slowly approached her with his familiar face. Yes, I can't imagine .. This is Boris .. has not changed. Her heart jumped and cried with joy ..

Maurice ran to Anna and muttered: "Darling, I've been waiting for you for a long time, my wife .. my age .."

Boris was returning from his visit to his parents' grave when he saw Anna, who did not erase time from her good. Al-Huwayna walks near his family nest, where they settled after the wedding for a few days, all that he had from Anna. None of them had enough dry sleep that night. They talked about all the events and harsh conditions that separated them. A hadith filled with sorrow, guilt and intense emotions.

Love at first sight

Boris first met Anna when he was the General Secretary of the Communist Party, giving a speech in the town of Provilika. Where a young woman, who was surrounded by her friends, listened with interest to his speech. Maurice did not take his eyes off her.

A rebellious and violent love relationship arose between them. Anna's family was one of the strongest opponents of the Communist Party, but Morris did not listen to critics. He said, "I liked it and I will always defend it. This is where the love story began. Maurice was absent from his homeland for a long time due to the nature of his work. They exchanged messages constantly. Anna is waiting for him when he returns from the army. In 1946, they married in a happy marriage, despite its simplicity. They got married despite the deteriorating financial situation and the harsh conditions of the war.

Separation

The couple spent only three days together until Boris returned to the army. That day Anna kissed him, saying goodbye, and it never occurred to her for a second that she would not meet him again until many years later.

After her husband left her, Anna lost touch and the government considered her an enemy of the people, like her father, and she was not spared repression. She was expelled with her family from her hometown in Siberia, leaving her entire life behind. She denied and ran away with her family without caring for her.

Boris returned from the army. Anna did not find his expectations, as usual, had no effect. The poor guy tried everything he could to find his young bride, but all his attempts were unsuccessful. He knocked on all the doors asking about them and no one knew where it went, and thus he lost every thread connecting him to him, as if the earth had been cracked open and consumed.

After their departure, Anna's mother planned to remarry her daughter and stated that Maurice was also married.

Anna said in a press interview, describing her suffering after leaving the family home, hated: "I told them I prefer suicide to leave because I can't live without Morris, but I have no cunning in my hands. It was one of the most difficult times in my life ... I miss him. I came back from work one day to check what was left of me from Morris. Unfortunately, I found that my mom burned his last letters, poems, photographs and even our wedding photos. She said that he forgot about me, so he didn't send the message. My mom told me that there is a man who wants to meet me, and I would be very lucky if he agreed to marry me. I drowned in tears and sorrow, I started tying my clothes in the form of a long rope and I was interested to hang myself, so my mom treated me with a strong slap in the face, cursing me, then she convinced me to marry Navid, she convinced me that it was my destiny. "

Thus, Anna got married and started a new life. Maurice was also married after desperate to find his lost love. But he did not forget Anna and wrote a book, which he gave to the woman who married him in her youth and spent only three nights with her. Morris said in a press interview, "Maybe I loved other women during our breakup, but Anna was my true love."

Link

Sometimes life is cruel and unfair, but sometimes it brings pleasant surprises. Today, 60 years later, fate unites them again.

Boris and Anna were widowed at the age of eighty. Both decided to return to their hometown. Where did they spend their childhood and youth days? The strange thing is that they both made the same decision on the same day and at the same time. Anna described her feelings at the moment when she met Morris: "I felt the same way as she felt the first time we met." ..

Boris insisted on marrying me. I was confused .. A bride at this age? And it was truly the happiest marriage of my life. Since we met again, there has been no dispute between us as we have been separated for a very long time and no one knows how much time we have left. We don't want to waste it on sterile spores. "

MARIA OKTYA PRSKAYA - A WOMAN WHO FOUGHT IN THE WAR IN REVENGE FOR HER HUSBAND

At one of the feminist meetings, thirty women in military uniform with a thick fur coat stood up and said: comrades from the National Association of Soldiers' Wives, it is a great honor for a woman to be the wife of a soldier who serves the country and sacrifices for him, but this is not enough for us, women who were honored by participating in the creation of this glory, I am the wife of an army officer and work as a soldier to protect the homeland, then she finished her speech with the applause of the women who were present at this meeting ..

This woman was nothing more than Maria Vasilyevna Oktia Perskaya, a simple village girl born on August 16, 1905 into a poor family in Crimea, who was struggling with a piece of bread with her ten brothers. Her parents were poor farmers who could barely provide a livelihood under the hunger and circumstances that took place in this country, However, Maria fought and worked in a cannery, and then moved to the city of Simferopol, where she worked as a telephone operator, and there she met a soldier The Red Army named Elia Rydenko both fell in love and got married in 1925 and decided to receive the title of Oktya Perska in honor of the Bolshevik revolution that took place in October 1917, and lived in a small hut on the outskirts of Kiev, and during this period Maria learned from her husband some policy issues and began to shoot well with a pistol

One night in 1941, the couple sat down at the dinner table and Maria noticed signs of worry on her husband's face, who was still on his mind.

- Honey, you haven't eaten your food, what's your concern?

I think the Nazi army is planning to invade our country.

- Impossible, because Nazi Germany is an ally of our country, and I even heard on the radio that our leadership sent several students to study in Germany.

- My dear Maria in politics, there is no friendship or constant enmity, there are suspicious movements at the borders, so I expect the war to start soon.

"Will you take part in the war, my dear.

Of course, I will participate in hostilities, since I am obliged as a soldier to defend my homeland.

Only a few months ago, the winter snow melted until the spark of war broke out on June 22. In 1941, Nazi forces invaded the territory of the Soviet Union as a result of a lightning military operation organized by Nazi leader Adolf Hitler Operation Barbarossa and 4 and a half million Nazi forces under supported by 600 thousand tanks, armored vehicles and a swarm of thousands of aircraft.

Maria found herself in the place of her beloved husband, who went to the battle fronts to defend his homeland, and after about two months of fighting, Ukraine is about to fall, and the authorities asked the residents of Kiev to leave for the city of Tomsk in Siberia in eastern Russia, Maria and her sister moved into the cold and cold desert of Siberia. She increased her suffering and fell ill with tuberculosis, and despite this, she worked as a nurse in the hospital to help the wounded who were very arriving at hospitals, especially after the national spirit of the Soviet people, which was surprised by the Nazi invasion, Maria very much hoped that her husband was captured and that he did not have it. He died in action, although she died a thousand times a day when she saw bodies and wounded arriving from the battlefronts with transport trucks and rushing to see if her husband was among them.

Two years after the outbreak of war, Maria learned that her husband had died while defending the city of Kiev in August 1941 AD. The news of his death threw away the old wound and sparked revenge on Mary, who vowed to avenge her husband and wore military clothes instead of mourning clothes, and I went to the recruiting headquarters of the Red Army and joined the ranks of people standing in long rows, but the evaluation committee declined Maria's request to join the army because she had tuberculosis and her age is not suitable, but she did not give up and thought of a strange idea when she sold her house and property AND her savings from her sewing and embroidery work until she collected 50 thousand rubles and returned to headquarters again and met with one of the officers responsible for registering recruits, and when she told him that she wanted to buy a tank to fight the Nazi invasion, he mocked her, indicated with his hand and asked her to go. to register with the ammunition manufacturing department, where women made ammunition or helped the wounded, while women were not allowed to fight in the front lines

Maria angered the headquarters and decided to write a letter to the high command asking to buy a tank and write in it: "To Comrade Joseph Stalin, I am a woman who lost her husband, who sacrificed his life in defense of the homeland. Please give me the honor to fight Nazi dogs, to avenge his death and death of innocent people under the barbaric torture of Nazi, I raised 50,000 rupees to buy a tank to fight the Nazi army. "She put the message in an envelope and sent it to the office of the President of the Soviet Union, Joseph Stalin, perhaps because of her anger, Maria didn't think anything at the time and laughed at herself when she calmed down. The explosion of her anger, and what happened was not taken into account. A few days later, an army officer knocked on her door and asked her to come to the recruiting headquarters. There, Maria was surprised that President Stalin agreed to her request to buy a tank, wishing her success in her combat missions

The approval came only to create propaganda and raise the morale of the fighters, so the woman never drove a tank at that time, and after paying the specified amount, Maria received a T-34 tank, which is a medium-sized tank, and it was decided to send her for military training at the Omsk military school, and it took 5 months to train. She completed the rank of tank commander in addition to learning the mechanical skills required to repair it, and in camp Maria became a tank commander and she wrote her "soldier-friendly" cannon on the turret, which caused ridicule among her associates and was transferred to the Panzer Corps in the Second Revolutionary Guard in preparation for the attack. The counter, which the Russian leadership called the Great Patriotic War to liberate the Eastern Front, and Maria participated in her first battle near the city of Smolensk on October 21, 1943 AD. She demonstrated her prowess by leading a tank with her four crew members and sending out strongholds of enemies, and managed to destroy a machine gun and an antitank pistol, a number of German soldiers were killed and promoted to the rank of sergeant.

A month later, on November 17, the Soviet army entered a fierce battle under cover of darkness. Tanks pushed forward to rebuild the town of Novy Selo near the town of Vitebsk. In complete darkness, a friendly battle tank split the ranks, and there was only the light of the shine of shells and the flame of fire from the nozzles of the cannons, Maria managed to hit hard and eliminate a number of enemy fortifications, but an artillery shell hit the tank. However, Maria did not surrender, jumped out of the tank, repaired the damage, and returned to battle until the city was liberated and she wrote a letter to her sister, which said: "I have taken revenge on my husband and it's time to avenge my homeland. "

After two months of continuous fighting, the Soviet leadership decided to launch a military campaign to liberate the city of Leningrad. On January 17, 1944, Soviet tanks launched a large-scale attack on the Shivdi village near Fatsback. Mary's tank was at the forefront, attacking enemy soldiers hid in destroyed houses and were able to destroy the movement's self-propelled weapons, Maria continued to advance into the center of the village in constant battle until she separated from the military convoy and was closely ambushed and shells poured on her tank from everywhere, causing the destruction of part of the tank shield and stopping movement

Maria ordered the tank crew to cover it with fire so that she could sneak up behind the tank to extinguish the fire and repair the engine, then she climbed onto the tank, and suddenly there was a huge explosion, and uncle smoked this place, and Maria fell into the room with tanks, and blood bleeding profusely from her head, and the team quickly left with the tank, and they took her to a field hospital, and then transferred to Vastovskaya hospital near Kiev, where doctors managed to remove a fragment that had penetrated her head, but Maria remained in a coma that lasted two months until she died on March 15, 1944 at the age of 38, and the Soviet leadership awarded her a bold medal of the first degree and was buried in one of the city squares, a memorial was erected to perpetuate her memory.

The war continued until the victory of the Soviet army and allies, and the Soviet flag was raised in the center of the German capital Berlin on May 2, 1945.

SEVERAL REASONS: THE HORSE'S REVENGE!

I think that Kenneth Bunyan's fatal accident is indeed one of the strangest and most surprising incidents, which is why it is always included in the list of the strangest deaths in history .. And I suspect that most people do not imagine the possibility of such incidents on the ground, but rather, some may not have heard of such questions at all, and here I am talking frankly about the problem of sex between humans and animals, especially with a horse! .. In the past, I wrote a detailed article about this type of anomaly called bestiality.

Kenneth Bunyan - 45 years old - worked as an engineer at Boeing for several years, married his sons. There is no evidence or indication in his appearance and public behavior that he is an eccentric. But there is a hidden and dark side to Kenneth's life that only a few of his close friends are aware of, who share the same abnormal tendencies and desires.

These gay friends tried everything to satisfy their homosexual obsession, so they seemed to no longer satisfy their desires and desires, except for the horse's penis! .. Their sick minds were severed in the devilish way that they trained horses to have sex with them. Not only that, they recorded these practices on tape, distributed them and posted them on the Internet. They often went to a large farm in Washington state to have sex with horses in their gardens. Of course this farm has obviously specialized in this and the best amateurs of all sides are forced to have sex with their different animals.

On July 2, 2005, there was a tragic accident while Kenneth and his companions were practicing their usual hobby on the farm, when the horse's penis burst so deep into Kenneth's body that he tore apart his colon and the accident was directly filmed by one of Kenneth's companions. ,.

At first, Kenneth and his companions thought it was easy, so they did not go to the hospital right away, but his condition worsened as a result of heavy bleeding, and when he was finally transferred to the hospital, the time was late and he soon died in the emergency room.

Kenneth's friend who transferred him to the hospital, left him there in the emergency room and escaped so that he would not be exposed, but police investigations soon reached him and he was arrested and through his investigation the importer was exposed, and the secret of the farm and the perverse and disgusting things that happen in her have been revealed.

Kenneth's bizarre death soon spread across the pages of newspapers and websites and sparked varying reactions between disgust, anger, sadness and irony, and this unique incident led to the passing of a law in Washington DC criminalizing animal sex.

WHEN THE TEACHER LOSES HER MIND

We have previously written extensively about male and female teachers who are sexually harassed by their students, and there are issues that are truly surprising, not only because it is a forbidden relationship between an adult, a minor, a teacher and a student, but because it carries great risk for the teacher, which includes job loss and scandal and contempt for people, which makes, in my opinion, an act of stupidity great. Rather, according to some researchers, it indicates a serious problem and a mental disorder.

One of the crazy women that the British press recently talked about a lot - English teacher Helen Trenball - 35 years old - this woman became her only concern, and her goal in life - her students yearn for her, to such an extent that the school administration scolded several times her for the sexy and see-through clothing she wears while teaching her students.

Helen's husband, 38 between Trenball, says he first met his wife in 2000 at a bar and felt very attracted to her and soon got married, and in 2001 they gave birth to their first child and their life was happy.

But soon after the wedding, a strange change began in Helen's behavior. Ben came home early from work one day to find the boys in his house, and when he went to the kitchen, he saw his wife in the arms of one of the boys holding hands and kissing. When the boy saw him, he ran away.

Helen and Ben had such a fight that day and Helen claimed that she went to buy a need, that she saw some of her students hanging out in the street and chatting with her, so she invited them to her home and she didn't nothing bad!.

Ben was so angry that he took the wedding ring off his hand, but later thought about his son, so he decided to forgive his wife.

As his wife's actions deteriorate, she began talking with admiration about one of her students, which made her husband feel uncomfortable. One day, he was returning home when Helen hinted that she was sitting in her car texting on her phone, and when he went to the window, he noticed on the phone the name of the boy you talked about a lot, and when Helen saw him, she immediately hid the phone, which made him angry and yelled at her, saying that her actions would lead to her being fired from her job in the end, then he went to her parents' house to complain about their daughter's behavior.

Helen's parents talked to her a lot, and under their influence she improved her behavior a little, but not for long, after a while she began to talk a lot about another boy from her fifteen-year-old students. She gave him private lessons with some of the students and she seemed very impressed with him.

The husband was convinced that his wife did not go to school to study, but for the admiration and thirst of students! .. He says: every morning she spent two hours getting ready, as if she was going to a party. I remember the day I wanted pants and a yellow shirt, her clothes were so transparent that her naked body was clearly visible. Helen directly told her husband to feel very enthusiastic about getting the boys' attention, and she was happy telling him how much they lost their feelings to the point that one of the boys touched her body during the lesson and was punished for a week from -for this. Ben says: I'm sure her happiness didn't help her because he did it.

Another time, a student wrote on the board: "Teacher Trenball is charming and delightful, I love her."

Ben says that he begged his wife a lot and fought a lot with her to change her behavior, but to no avail, and he was very afraid of the feelings of his son, who is studying in the same director

In 2009, Helen gave birth to a baby girl and her baby's life calmed down a bit, but Helen soon returned to sexy clothes and a long time out of the house. One day Ben returned home and found that his wife was wearing a very short skirt and her underwear was clearly visible, she said that she would go to sleep with some of her friends in the apartment for fun, but between him refused, he was sure that she going to have sex with one of her students, In the end, she didn't go, but they quarreled violently, and in the morning she took the children and left the house.

It was clear that the family life between them was over, and soon divorce, custody of the children and, ultimately, their profit between the children and the children who returned to live with him began between them.

After Elena broke up with her husband and everyone knew about her abnormal behavior, her beloved student began to try to break off relations with her, but she did not leave him, but she drove her car every night to park her near his house. just to see him and all the neighbors heard the boy's father come out to her and yell at her because she was chasing his son and called the police who arrested her. Helen appeared in court on juvenile relations charges, admits she exchanged kisses and scandalous text messages with him, but she denied sleeping with him and the court sentenced her to four months in prison and did not allow her to engage in any activities with children and minors, which means preventing her from teaching for the rest of her life.

Ben took his son out of school after Helen was exposed and he feared the rest of the students would lend him to his mother. The most common thing about Ben is his daughter, a child who misses his mother very much but does not want any relationship with Helen, who is believed to have schizophrenia, when she is not stalking students, she is normal, but her love for teenagers destroyed her ...

Helen, apparently, was not very upset about the separation from her husband and children, because she soon entered into a relationship with another of her students.

It's a shame that there is a teacher or teacher with this harsh and recklessness, but Helen is not unique. There are a significant number of scandalous problems in the world that are spread by newspapers and satellite channels and whose teachers are their heroes..

Finally, what do you think, dear reader, about this behavior? .. Is it a mental illness or a late teenager? .. Have you ever experienced such models of male and female teachers with abnormal and perverse behavior ??.

WHAT DO YOU KNOW ABOUT MARRIAGE, SOLO?

Marriage in its traditional sense is a relationship between a man and a woman, but in recent years we have heard of other types of marriage, such as men marrying men and women with women. Although most people object to gay marriage, I find it more understandable than the type of marriage that I would like to talk to you about .. It is a man's marriage in itself, since I do not know what it means for a man to marry himself. although I don't mind that.

Proponents of marriage or single marriage (Sologamy) say this maximizes human love for oneself and self-acceptance .. but why? .. Are there people who hate themselves? .. Yes .. A large group of people seems to be unconvincing in themselves, be it in form, appearance, work and action .. And the lack of self-love can turn into a closed tendency and a lower node, rather, this dissatisfaction with oneself, according to psychologists, is the basis of most psychological problems and therefore single marriage is a form of treatment because it emphasizes the value of one, and thus leads to a more convincing and happier life.

There are also those who see in one marriage a form of cynicism and cynical opposition to traditional marriage, especially for those who have experienced bad relationships, as if their language says: "Being alone is better and safer than puzzling over marriage and its problems. . ".

In turn, those who object to single marriage say that this is all just a pathetic show of a desperate person, and that this is a type of narcissism that can lead to self-reliance and, therefore, isolation, withdrawal and depression. And this is mostly without meaning or purpose, so it means spending a lot of money on having a lavish wedding that invites your friends and family to marry yourself, where is the logic to travel first class to a tourist resort for your honeymoon? .. And book a full hotel room to spend the night by going in with you! .. Who knows .. Fate may have helped you have children with you! ..

Other protesters say marriage alone is a gimmick or vehicle to gain attention and promote oneself, especially as marriage marriages are getting modern and the local press may be writing about it.

But for most of those who marry themselves, the objection of the protesters does not mean anything, after all, it is personal freedom, as long as what they do does not harm any other person, and for this reason the number of people entering in one marriage, is increasing, especially among women, as we teach a woman an emotional character, so a wedding suit and a wedding party is almost the focus of many girls' dreams from an early age. The fact that some celebrities contracted this marriage and shed some light on it with flags has contributed to a numerical boom, and this coincided with the emergence of companies and agencies specializing in organizing solo weddings, as this is an area that shows steady growth year after year.

Perhaps the strangest thing about one marriage is that some people have merged a lot during the wedding ceremony, which is why you see the groom address himself in influential terms like, "I forgive myself for everything."! .. And "From now on I will not call myself ugly." .. And "I am pleased with myself and do not blame her for anything." .. And "I will forget the past and turn a new page." .. Some of them may be involved crying, as if it were a kind of frankness and reconciliation with oneself.

What do you know about single marriage?

Chinese Liu Yi spoke about his marriage to himself in 2007, saying, "I am not gay, as some might think, I do not deny that I am a little narcissistic, but my main goal in my marriage is to dismantle and rebuild myself. I want to use this wedding to reconsider a marriage of the opposite sex. My behavior may sound silly, but I am a traditional person, and therefore I wanted to arrange a traditional wedding, which I called the people of my city. ".

Of course, for most of the townspeople this did not seem traditional or understandable, especially when the groom entered the hall with his bride, the bride was only a form of strength for the groom and he was wearing a traditional Chinese wedding dress !. One of the old men commented on what was happening, saying: "What's going on here .. Who's getting married ?!" Another guest said, trying to hide his laughter: "This is the strangest wedding I've ever attended." .. While another guest criticized what was happening and considered it proof that the groom suffers from psychological problems, because for a man in the mid-thirties, it is not normal not to look for a partner for your life.

As for the Italian fitness trainer Laura Messi, her solo marriage took place on the basis of a decision she made a long time ago to get married if she turns forty, without finding the right and right man to bond with. And since she did not find this promised person, so she decided to continue the wedding and invited seventy people from her relatives and friends, and spent a large amount on supplies, requirements and wedding details, while the honeymoon was a wonderful trip to Egypt.

The funny thing is that Laura told the local newspaper that if she found the right man, she would want to divorce and marry him !. "If I ever find someone with whom I can plan my future, I will be happy, but my happiness will not depend on him." I firmly believe that each of us should love ourselves first. Anyone can live in a fairytale atmosphere even without a prince. This is my fabulous wedding, but without the handsome Prince Charming. ".

Of course, not everyone who marries themselves does this because they have not found a suitable partner, rather that the opposite may be true, as some marry as an expression of celebration and happiness for getting out of a failed love relationship or an unhappy marriage, like in the case of British Sophia Tanner, who speaks of her only marriage: "Everyone celebrates bonding with someone and getting married, but there is no sign in society that you are avoiding the horrible thing or returning to your own happiness and contentment."

It is worth noting that no country in the world legally recognizes or considers same-sex marriage at the level of personal transactions. I come back and say that I personally do not see any harm in a man marrying himself as long as it does not affect another person other than him, but on the other hand, I do not find any meaning for this marriage, except for the symbolic side, but a realist in general doesn't make sense because if

I take myself as an example, be a single man older than me and I assumed I would marry myself, which would change from my life! .. I mean, I'm sitting alone in my damn room right now. Does my marriage to myself mean that there will be another person or partner in the room? .. And this person is just me !!. I mean, even at the phrasing level, it seems silly.

In general, I congratulate everyone who is satisfied and confident in themselves, I sincerely hope that everyone is reconciled with themselves, and I am the first of them. In conclusion, I can only ask you about your opinion, dear reader, in this type of marriage. Do you consider it healthy, which helps to strengthen and build yourself, or is it just messing around, hypocrisy and wasting time and money ?.

THE STRANGEST ANOMALY

For most people, homosexuality is associated with same-sex relationships, that is, male attraction for men and women for women, but in practice, homosexuality has been removed from the list of homosexuality since the 1970s, and in contrast, every year new types are added to the list of homosexuality. (Paraphilia) While it does not include things that most people may not think about and cannot believe in its existence, but the human psyche remains the mother of miracles and strange things on this planet.

Of course, I will not dwell on the question of the definition of homosexuality and its causes, because there is a clear difference between the scientists themselves in this regard, but in short and simply we can say that anomaly is imagination, attraction, arousal and sexual behavior associated with abnormal things. in the eyes of most people. As for its causes, there is a great deal of scientific debate about it, most of the theories and research focus on childhood and adolescence, especially when sexual stimulation in early adolescence, or the onset of masturbation, is associated with a particular thing, such as stimulation resulting from the suffering or crying of others. or to be beaten and insulted, often remains This connection exists until the end of a person's life and turns into an anomaly. The environment also influences the occurrence of these deviations. For example, a recent study concluded that men who have older siblings have a larger anomaly.

In this article, we will briefly touch on some of the strangest types of anomalies, purpose and purpose, as we discussed earlier in our articles, that address sexual issues that do not provoke instincts and desires as strongly as identifying readers with these things that may come across them in their life, or they may notice them in the behavior of people close to them Or, when they themselves, but they do not know who they are, and they may consider them normal ..

1 - Thirst for tears and crying (Dacryphilia) Sexual arousal is stimulated when an injured person is seen when he sees another person crying or crying, and there are two types of this anomaly, the first is sadistic, that is, the victim feels motivated when he sees how others cry as a result of the suffering he has caused, like a husband who harms his wife and feels sexual stimulation and ecstasy when you see him cry or in pain. The second type The victim does not cause the opposite person to cry, not the other way around, he may express sympathy and try to find good thoughts, but nevertheless, the tear in the eyes of the interviews causes him to lust and motivates him sexually.

2 - Ghosts and Genie's Thirst (Spectrophilia): First of all, I would like to say, and since my site is full of stories about Genie's lover, I never say that the owners of these stories have some anomalies, their stories may be true, but here I am talking about what scientists say - and God remains primarily science and the world - according to these scientists, the feeling of sexual arousal as a result of imagining a relationship with a non-human being or entity, such as genies and ghosts, is a type of anomaly and it is widespread. affects both men and women, and has nothing to do with suppression or sexual deprivation, as it can happen to famous people and artists, and countless stories

around the world spread around him.

3- Nismophilia: Sexual arousal or stimulation as a result of tickling or tickling others. Of course, this is not a condition that the business is happening with the bed partner, but it can happen by accident, for example, someone may ask you to tickle him, or you tickle someone as a joke and suddenly notice that he is aroused or sexually disturbed. and vice versa, that is, someone tickles you. You feel excited. In one of the documented cases, one of the young people said that his beloved's sister asked him to tickle her as a joke, and once, when he tickled her, he noticed excitement and ecstasy at her, hugged him and accepted him, then she apologized to him later, and the case was repeated twice later, and it always involved tickling.

4 - Menophilia: This is a man's urge to menstruate in women, or rather his sense of arousal and motivation to see menstrual blood, and even his smell and taste! .. The injured person can be easily distinguished from his behavior, as he feels great euphoria when having sex with a woman during the menstrual cycle.

5 - Elderly Cravings (Gerontophilia): The admiration or desire of men or women, for those who are older than them, is not an anomaly, but an anomaly is the cravings of older women over sixty years of age or more, for example, in one of the cases documented at the beginning of the last century, a young man at the age of twenty threw his young wife Belle on her wedding night and went to sleep in the arms of a 64-year-old woman .. This, of course, is an anomaly, and it is strange that its prevalence is not small, one of the recent Research has found that a small percentage of pornographic visitors have this type of anomaly.

6 - Abdominal Gas Bullying (Eproctophilia) You might think this is a joke, dear reader, and I'm sorry if it disgusts you, but

there are actually people with this abnormality who get sexually aroused when their partner secretes in bed. gases (fart) One of the wounded said that he feels delighted when he is with a beautiful woman, and blows in front of him in a disgusting loud voice !. Some people feel euphoric when they smell bad abdominal gas.

7 - Bullying vomiting (Emetophilia): Feelings of excitement and motivation when an injured person is vomiting or vomiting in bed or in a relationship. While most people experience nausea or discomfort when they see vomiting or vomiting, a person with this anomaly reaches a peak of happiness and ecstasy when vomiting others in front of him or him, and may feel more ecstatic if he is vomiting !.

NOTE .. WHEN LOVE IS AN ILLUSION

He loves me. He loves me not.

One of the doctors told him that one of the patients came to him complaining that he had communicated through a social networking site with one of the famous Hollywood stars and that she confessed to him that he had fallen in love with him and wanted to be together .. Let the doctor finds out later that she not only does not love him, as he claimed, but does not even know him! But this patient somehow managed to translate every publication and every comment that the actress places on her page as an expression of love and passion, hidden by encrypted messages addressed to him, even though it was only a public page where the actress exchanged topics and comments with their fans, as is usually the case ..

But when the doctor confronted him with the truth, he could not accept it or try to convince him of it, but at best he angrily wondered that if it was really true, then why did he lead him to this feeling towards her?

In psychiatry, which adheres to the false illusion that another person (usually a famous figure) is in love with you under the name "Antromania" or "de Clerambault syndrome" compared to its discoverer Gaitan Gatian De Clerambault in 1985 ... And this is the question of such hallucinations accumulates his imaginary interest, so that the situation turns from mere belief or hallucinations into famous sightings that have happened to several celebrities over the years, such as Judy Foster, David Letterman, Kiara Knightley, Madonna, Sandra Bullock ... some ended tragically, as happened to the Latin pop star Slenia Perez, who was killed by a crazy fan gunned down in a small hotel room.

Although the name Antromnia or de Clerambo was officially named for this phenomenon in 1985, it has been documented since the ancient Greek era, when Hippocrates described and said it a thousand years ago. Also, a hundred years ago, I documented the case of a patient, Antromania, who stood near Buckingham Palace, looking at the room of King George V, fascinated by his every movement, even if the poor man pulled the window curtain to see or breathe a little fresh air, where she directly translated his intuitive movement as a clear declaration of his love for her ... He also did not mention this phenomenon in the description of the five cases reported by a French psychiatrist in 1921, sixty-four years before the case, which de Clerambault attributed to himself.

Social media has inadvertently contributed to this type of delusion where the patient imagined a man or woman who fell in love with him in one way or another, just a passing comment on that character, an image he uploaded to his account, or a post I wrote on her page. ...

The patient may receive personal information about his package, perhaps due to her unhappiness, he reached it to end up in a coffin with the police or her.

This phenomenon can occur due to psychological pressure, inherited genes, trauma, stroke, cerebral hemorrhage, dementia, or any type of nervous disorder that may be associated with a defect in the frontal lobe of the brain (frontotemporal lobe).).

While some associate them with a number of syndromes classified under the heading of non-identification syndromes, such as Capgrass syndrome (in which the injured suffer from the misconception that people have been replaced by a charlatan) and Friguli syndrome (in which a person thinks that one person controls appearance and personality several other people). This means that it is closely related to a defect in facial identification in front of you, which is scientifically associated with injuries to the right side of the brain.

Proof of this is that a person with this condition makes the mistake of identifying love that is essentially missing by reading facial expressions or nodding at a victim's picture posted on the Internet or general social interaction with little ability to understand what you really think or feel. Simply put, he thinks that the person loves him and he really doesn't notice his existence in the first place. It does not distinguish between the subtle thread that separates the insistence on getting the attention of the person you love and falling into the burden of being stalked, stalked, and stalked through illness to end up in jail. Perhaps it was only a one-sided relationship in his search for his life partner, which at some point deviated to become very extreme.

This phenomenon often affects women in relation to an older man of outstanding social status and to a lesser extent and in the earliest stages of men in relation to an attractive young woman, but the difference is that the person is jealous of his imaginary lover for persecution or any other illegal violation. That is, he adopts the same model as the natural mating behavior of males and females, and while he is replete with females by nature, the most famous of her condition were her male heroes due to her dramatic goals!

It is no secret that natural mutual love, before it received a response from the other side, was once at the stage of development of one-sided relations, i.e. delusion from him before he became his partner and accepted him to exchange the same feelings. Or this phenomenon may take on another element in the form of a husband or wife who does not feel emotionally sufficient towards his partner, so he begins to deceive himself that he has a very different relationship or that his wife is even better than him .. Or that her husband or his wife loves him more than he loves her .. These subconscious entromanic delusions can be exaggerated, but at times are important in maintaining the continuity of good friendships .. You or I can mislead some things from time to time .. Does not lead to damage.

Okay, what's the difference between starting this normal relationship and deviating from the degree of entromania? ..

An entromnia patient tends to follow harassment and constant harassment behavior by sending text messages, emails, phone calls, and even gifts sometimes .. Every effort is also made to acquire all of his lover's or his lover's related films from films, magazines, photographs and books in his painstaking search for any encrypted messages addressed to him.

So how can I tell it from any other delusional disorder ??

Psychologists agreed that there are five diagnostic characteristics and differences between entromnia and other mental disorders such as schizophrenia, bipolar disorder, and Alzheimer's disease:

* Strange misconceptions continue for a month or more.

* Despite the delusion, schizophrenia has not been diagnosed and ruled out with routine tests.

* The victim's overall performance and behavior were not impaired as in the case of Alzheimer's.

* Obsession or depression is short compared to the duration of delusions.

* Finally, these misconceptions cannot be attributed to the physiological effects of a substance, other disease, or any other mental disorder.

Once it is confirmed that the person is indeed infected with de Clerambault syndrome, placebo treatment can be difficult because those affected cannot deal with the fact that their beliefs are unfounded. Relatively few of them can seek treatment on their own. Treatment should also address the needs of any individual who is traumatized separately, such as maintaining his social work, reducing his problem behaviors, and ensuring an improvement in his quality of life through social life education and helping to solve his problems arising from future sexual libido. ... Focus on medication for underlying disorders, while ensuring that those affected follow an agreed recovery plan and communicate their illness. Sometimes a patient may be forced to enter a clinic if the doctor considers it dangerous to himself or others. Fortunately, the rate of treatment without relapse is very high with this type of sexual deviation.

www.ingramcontent.com/pod-product-compliance
Lightning Source LLC
Chambersburg PA
CBHW051957150726
47999CB00004B/1418